PRAISE FOR

THE
FIRES

"This work is—as Chekov said—informed by the deeper harmonies. When Alan Cheuse writes, 'she is retreating from desire but not from love,' it is as if the woman suffering from this relentless condition has just entered the room. *The Fires* offers the twin bequeathing of profound sadness and enchantment. Cheuse is a writer of immense gifts."
   —Howard Norman (author of *Devotion* and *The Bird Artist*)

"With intelligence and wit, Alan Cheuse takes us through the searing, tragic, heart-breaking and hilarious business of being alive. The two novellas that make up *The Fires*—one of sorrow and one of radiance—are filled with characters trying to maneuver that space between creation and destruction. Some come to ashes and some find forgiveness—even for themselves. Through it all, Cheuse never betrays the dignity or humanity of his characters. His brilliant creations are in good hands right to the end, as are we."
                    —Ana Menendez (author of *Loving Che* and
                              In Cuba I was a German Shepherd)

"Alan Cheuse is one of the most engaged and vital writers on the scene today."
   —Robert Stone (author of *Dog Soldiers* and *A Flag for Sunrise*)

This copy of some novellas — for ready please (I hope) and win Mets for her own win —

THE
FIRES

ALAN CHEUSE

[signature]

5/8/0?

D.C.

sf(WP)
SANTA FE WRITERS PROJECT

literary **nd**

investing in literature
one book at a time

providing a foundation
for writers around the globe

www.literaryventuresfund.org

Library of Congress Control Data

Cheuse, Alan
The Fires/by Alan Cheuse

ISBN 13: 9780977679911
ISBN:10: 0977679918
Fiction

Library of Congress Control Number: 2006939320

Cover design by Bill Douglas at The Bang
Printed and bound in Canada

Visit SFWP's website: www.sfwp.com and literary journal: www.sfwp.org

TRANS   10 9 8 7 6 5 4 3 2 1

For Kris

THE FIRES

1.

The worst news always comes at the worst possible moment. In Gina's case, this happened to be while she was squatting over the commode in the upstairs bathroom, attempting to catch a urine sample for Dr. Betsy Cohen. She felt so ridiculous, the weeks of hot and cold flashes, the upswings and downturns of mood, the deep and nearly debilitating sense of longing for Paul, and then long stretches of absolute indifference, even—oh, this may just have been the worst of it all before the telephone rang—even wishing, yes, that he might stay away a while longer.

This was, in fact, Gina's third try at catching a sample.

Steady, steady, she was saying to herself. I can fix a perfect Bloody Mary on demand, I know exactly when I begin to ovulate—or used to—and I can flip a pancake in a thirty-mile-an-hour wind—remembering that lovely camping trip they had taken in the Sierra just after a visit to Paul's mother in Sacramento—but I can't seem to collect pee in a vial.

Actually, on her first attempt, she had done it perfectly, scarcely splashing anything on her fingers and hand. But then it turned out that she had forgotten whether or not the collection had been of her first urination of the day or her second. She was supposed to save a sample of her second. And she was almost sure this had been it. Except that she had a vague recollection of waking in the early dawn light and staggering into the bathroom. Or could that have been the morning before? Or might it have been a dream? Paul had come to her in the night, pulling a red wagon, the kind that small boys use to deliver sand to their neighbors while pretending that it is gold. Nothing portentous in that, yes? Then the dream changed, a wall of darkness became a scrim of rain, and there was her father—years since she had dreamed of him—in deep conversation with her first husband, and try as she might, Gina could not make out anything they said. Funny, how she had strained to listen, immediately forgetting the sight of Paul.

The second try? She had gotten the timing right, she had peed in a jiffy into the container, and then, as she was putting the thing away in the freezer to store while she waited the appropriate time according to the instructions for collection of her saliva samples, she dropped the little collection vial, spilling some of her urine onto the kitchen counter.

And now wait, here she was, just about to finish this third time, her pants down around her ankles, her skirt rucked up into her lap, tangy liquid gushing out of her, her knuckles damp but her mind focused—when the telephone rang.

Damn!

A few moments of comedy as she stood up, spraying her underwear, her skirt, the bathroom mat, the tile floor, and struggled to adjust her clothes even as she dropped the vial onto the mat and staggered out of the bathroom and sent herself stumbling toward the telephone on the bedside table. She was thinking this wouldn't happen to Paul, he takes the portable telephone into the bathroom with him. Which made her laugh out loud.

And then—more comedy—the doorbell rang—she would never know who it was at the door, because after a while they stopped ringing—just as she picked up the telephone.

"Hello?" she said, hoping, of course, that it was Paul. She would tell him immediately about her immediate circumstances, squatting, aiming herself at the vial. He would—

"Missus Morgan?"

Thick accent, something out of Russia? Did she know a Russian? Did she know someone in Russia?

"Yes?"

Satellite delay, the connection fading in and out. This feeling of telephone limbo, an awful by-product of modern life. Sometimes Gina told herself that she might have been better off born into an earlier age. Just when that might have been, she couldn't figure. Sometime when—?

"Missus Morgan, This is Mohammed Kirov. Your husband's—"

It wasn't that she cut him off, it was just the satellite delay made her overspeak his voice.

"I know who you are, yes," Gina said. "Paul has often—"

And then the same thing happened to her as happened to him.

"—assistant," Kirov said. *"Here in Uzbekistan, the roads—"*

"—spoken about you. But why—?"

"—[words faded out] *traveling, you understand—?"*

"Why are you calling? Where's—"

Silence at the other end, nothing there at all except the slight echoing in and out of the reflection of the silence in the space between here and some point above the Earth, or along the line where her voice bounced back down on his side of the globe.

"Missus Morgan?" Suddenly his voice returned, stronger than before, emphatic, almost as though he had something to sell her or a message of great importance and he stood just outside the door to the room demanding to be let in.

And then of course it came to her, and as if this Kirov, or some other man, an intruder bent on wounding her, pounding away at her, raping her, killing her, had smashed in the door and pushed her down beneath it, she felt all the air leave her lungs and she staggered back onto the bed, feeling the dampness between her legs, the legacy of comedy, but the comedy had ended.

On the flight east, she had plenty of time—many times the time—to reenact the incident in her mind. The medication that Dr. Betsy had prescribed for her a few weeks ago, just after Paul had left on the first leg of this trip, hadn't kicked in, or it wasn't strong enough a dose. Her departure from home was just too hurried for her to worry about such things. But when she settled back in the leather seat after takeoff—luckily, she had gotten a place in first class, a combination of her frenzied state when she appeared at the airport and a sympathetic clerk behind the ticket counter—and God help you that you need such things to happen to you in order to travel in this manner—she knew that the trip was going to be the most difficult of her life.

Turbulence over the Atlantic didn't bother her. Dishes rattled, other passengers spoke in harried whispers, unable to sleep through the frightening bounces and jamming in air. She was awake, alert, and in her mind going over and over again the incident as Kirov had described it to her.

First of all, Paul wouldn't have been drunk. It had been two years since he had stopped drinking and there was no reason in the world—none, at least, that she could at first imagine, and her imagination was certainly racing along at least as fast as the jet she was flying in—that would lead him to start again.

But then she tried to picture it, and suddenly, on the wings of this awful euphoria—the only way that she could describe it—of delusion in which you would think anything in the world no matter how illogical if it would bring him back to you—it didn't seem all that preposterous that he could have perhaps taken one, maybe two, drinks. He was alone, tired, why not?

The flight attendant came up the aisle, smiled, showing beautiful white teeth, the kind Paul always admired. (Gina had off-white teeth and always felt a little uneasy when Paul would point out the brilliant smile of even a particularly plain woman whom they might encounter.) What if he had met a woman with a smile like that? What if she had sat next to him? That might have led him to ask the flight attendant for a Bloody Mary, his old favorite. So what if he had one or two? He hadn't ever been an alcoholic, he just drank too much. And he had decided to stop. On a long flight, the same flight that she was on the first leg of, any man might have succumbed to the urge to make himself comfortable.

(But why wasn't she drinking? She always enjoyed a drink, fixing at least one of those perfect Bloody Marys for herself for every two he drank. Why wasn't she drinking? She couldn't say. Well, yes, she could. Why lie to herself? The alcohol would combine with the tranquilizer and knock her out. She didn't want oblivion. She wanted to stay awake, to think about him.)

Paul had arrived late on the flight from Moscow. A foolish thing, to go through Moscow, but he had not been there for several years and wanted to see all of the fabled changes he had heard about, the markets overflowing with fruit from the south, the new boutiques, the flashy dressers on the street, herds of big expensive new cars. And of course he had wanted to see their old apartment. That thing he had for history, personal, public. It was just a hobby, nothing at all to do really with how he earned his living. But it was all-consuming. Digging about in his family's past, pressing her for the details of her own past. Keeping a notebook. What if they had had children? (Well, a child who had lived…) That might have turned his eye toward the future rather than the past. Maybe. But when you consider the way friends of theirs who did have children kept such methodical records, photographic and otherwise, of their childrens' lives, Paul would probably have done the same, making notes of everything from—where did it begin?—first breath and first bowel movement, on to first steps, first words, and beyond.

Gorky Street, across from one of the big tourist hotels. Seventh floor, with a wonderful view across the Kremlin and the river. The apartment had belonged to a mid-level Party official, who had somehow managed to sell it to Paul's company during that ephemeral time when Gorbachev's people were talking about deals they wanted to make with western companies but no one was putting anything on paper.

"The government's just like this apartment," Paul had said. "They want to air it out, but the windows are stuck."

"It certainly smells like every head of cabbage they boiled."

"Gina, these were privileged Party people," Paul said. "If they boiled anything in here, it would have been artichokes imported all the way from California." He laughed his hearty laugh and went out the door. Gina opened a window and leaned out over the street seven stories below and watched as he exited the building and followed his progress along the sidewalk until he was lost in the crowd.

With Paul at his meetings, she used the time to explore. That is what wives of American engineers did, wasn't it? Moscow was then still a safe city and with her British-bought rain slicker concealing her obviously American clothes, she could walk the streets and ride the metro without people paying her too much attention. So she floated silently through flea markets and half-filled shops, to small museums and even to the wretched Moscow zoo where most of the animals looked like refugees from happier zones.

In front of the compound where the ammoniac odor of the big cats was so overwhelming that she felt her knees begin to give, a man caught her by the shoulder.

He said something in Russian.

"I don't speak…" Gina turned around. He was middle-aged, with a day's growth of white beard, and wore jeans and an oddly made denim jacket.

"Are you all right?" the man asked in French.

She nodded, thanked him, took a quick look at the two ragged tigers lying there on the filthy rocks, and walked away.

She couldn't wait until Paul came back that night, even if it was only to hustle her out the door to a business dinner at the city's most famous Central Asian restaurant. There was a British couple from the corporation and several Russian men, all of them absolutely polite even after they had run through the table's fourth bottle of Hungarian red. There was music from an accordion player and a guitarist, with a young girl who played the flute and a boy, who could have been her brother, tapping on small drums and clinking tiny tin cymbals.

"Our American partner," said one of the Russians, a young man with long hair curling over his ears and a suit that to Gina's eye appeared to have cost more than Paul's. He raised his glass.

The couple from London did the same.

By the time they finished toasting, they had emptied two more bottles of the red.

"And do you find our city interesting?" The other Russian spoke. He was older, and portly, clean-shaven and smelling of expensive western cologne.

"I went to the zoo," Gina said.

"There is zoo here?" the younger Russian said.

The older man looked at him with a piteous glance.

"It's a filthy place," the British woman said.

"We're rebuilding," the portly Russian said. "And thanks to people such as Paul Morgan, the good things will come faster."

"Who goes to this zoo?" the younger Russian asked.

"Families," the portly man said.

"Yes," Gina said, "there were families there."

"Do you and Paul have any children?" The British woman hovered closer to her.

"No," Gina said, looking at Paul. "Well…no…"

Paul might have been about to speak, but the young Russian businessman had a question.

"Perhaps there is money to be made in zoo?"

The older man laughed.

"Selling off the seals by the pound?"

Gina had a flickering thought about the unshaven but courteous man at the tiger pit, and then asked the British woman about her family. And with that wonderful manner of his, within a minute or two Paul got them all laughing again. She was very proud of him and pleased that she had decided to take two weeks away from her job at the museum in order to accompany him on this trip. But then she had for years wanted to see him in action on the road. It was a memory that no one could take away from her, ever.

When they returned to the apartment after the meal Gina imagined she caught a whiff of the rank scent of the big, bedraggled cats—this didn't blend well with the lingering traces of the artichokes or whatever they had cooked here. She was suddenly sorry that they had eaten such hot food. And then she took the taste of Paul's mouth in hers, and a wonderfully dreamy half hour of love-making followed, flavored with Central Asian spices.

Had Paul remembered some of it when he passed through the city this time? He might have been too busy. The firm had a large office in the city center and the same portly Russian, or so Paul had explained it to her over the telephone before he left on his flight to Tashkent, was now the chief executive officer of an entirely new configuration of oil and gas interests, something as close to a subsidiary of the American corporation as you could get under the current Russian laws. While she listened to Paul, she could hear the noises of a busy office in the background.

"How has it been for you?" he asked.

"I was up all night again," she said, trying, while she spoke, to figure the time difference between them.

"The same problems?"

"Yes," she said. "Terrible hot flashes."

"I'm sorry," he said. "Are you doing anything for it?"

"I've got an appointment with Betsy Cohen," she said. "She wants to run some tests on me. So she can see if it's actually happening."

"Good scientific approach," he said.

"Paul," she said.

Then paused.

"Yes?"

"I can't even begin to talk calmly about this. It is driving me crazy."

"Sorry," he said.

"You keep saying that," she said.

"Sorry. Sorry! What else am I supposed to say?"

"I don't know," she said. "Maybe I better hang up."

"Not just yet," he said. "Tell me about your day."

"Not a bad day," she said. "I just feel sort of blah. It's the nights, Paul."

"The nights," he said.

"The nights."

"I'm sorry I'm not there to comfort you," he said.

"Don't feel sorry," she said. "If you were here, you would feel worse. Because you couldn't comfort me."

"It's that bad?"

"That's what I'm trying to tell you. Yes."

Pause at his end of the line.

"I haven't been getting a great deal of sleep myself."

"Late meetings?"

"That. And passing through these time zones. I've already been out and back once since we last spoke, you know."

"You have?"

"Yes, a quick trip to Alma Ata and back again."

"'Out and back,'" she said. "That would give me a headache. On top of my headache."

"I don't have a headache. I'm just a bit tired. I hope to get some sleep on the plane to Tashkent, but you never can tell about those flights."

"About any flights," she said.

"Right," he said.

"So," she said.

"When are you going to see the doctor?"

"I told you, I'm having these tests."

"What exactly are they?"

"Urine samples, saliva samples."

A pause at his end of the line.

"I'd like to sample your saliva," he said.

"Oh, you would?"

"I would," he said. "As soon as I get back I'll conduct some tests on you myself."

Gina felt it then, a touch of heat at the back of her legs and heat running in slender threads up toward her buttocks.

"I'll be in the waiting room, Doctor," she said.

"The nurse will be with you in a minute," he said.

She couldn't stand it.

"I have to go," she said.

"All right," he said. "Will you be at home tomorrow night?"

"Yes, I think so."

"I'll call you from the airport at Tashkent. Before I drive off into the desert."

"Paul of Arabia," she said. "My hero. Be careful."

"I'll be fine. You're the one I worry about."

"Don't worry about me," she said. "I'll be fine."

Pause.

"Doctor?"

"Nurse," he said right back to her.

Just at that moment another voice came on the line, speaking in Russian.

"Paul?" Gina said.

"Crossed lines," he said as the other voice faded away.

"Be careful," she said.

"No danger, stiff upper lip, tribes in that region are all pacified."

"I love you," she said, that heat running up and down her legs.

"I love you, too," he said. "Bye."

She was jolted awake by turbulence, the airplane descending down a hill of layered air as it made the first approach, according to the captain who spoke over the intercom, to the Frankfurt airport. My first approach, she said to herself, has not been very successful. Slumped in a chair in the waiting area, she slid over the edge of sleep.

2.

He had arrived late on the flight from Moscow, yes. And he was tired, but not any more than the usual discomfort after an overnight flight from Dulles, compounded by a night of eating heavy and drinking hard with the company people. It was the insertion into his schedule of this trip to Alma Ata that added the extra poundage of fatigue. Outbound, he couldn't sleep because of the turbulence. He always told himself that it was just like riding a motor boat that was skipping over rough water. Intellectually that made it seem like a simple thing. But there was just no way that he could find to doze off while they were bumping around up there. And then another heavy meal with some government officials in that mountain city before heading back to the airport and waiting for his return flight to Moscow. Ridiculous that he couldn't just make the short hop over to Tashkent, but there was a full day of meetings in Moscow between him and Uzbekistan.

And then things began to go wrong, not terribly wrong, but just enough to put him on edge. The company driver who took him back to the airport offered a shortcut through a neighborhood of cement block shacks, and they no sooner had turned the corner off the main avenue when one of their tires went flat. Paul had had to wait there in the dark, inhaling the smell of gasoline, standing water—there were puddles all around though it had not rained that day—and the odor of a dozen cooking fires, while smoking his first cigarette in two years. He cadged it from the embarrassed driver and felt a little silly himself. What would he tell Gina? He told her everything, but then most of what he reported in the last few years had been good things, and if not good, then at least merely trivial, not degrading like this, giving in to his old habit.

The air was cold up here, and he smoked harder, as if it might warm him a bit. I should find one of those cooking fires and stand close to it, he told himself. Imagine, a stranger, a westerner, American no less, going up to one of these little cement shanties and knocking on the door. Well, he knew they would be hospitable and invite him in. And he would be offered the meal they had been counting on for their next day's fare.

His mouth watered. He was hungry. His bowels gurgled and pitched as he sucked in more smoke, held it...exhaled into the dark.

"How are you doing?" he said to the driver.

The man looked up from his labor at the front of the car, but said nothing.

Paul pictured what it would be like in this part of town, all over the city, in fact, if the project went through. Better light! Better energy! All across these dark and ominous mountain nations, people could begin to live a different life.

As if to mock his thought at the time, an old woman came limping up the lane, pulling something behind her. It took a moment before Paul could make it out, some kind of wagon, it seemed to be at first. But the closer she got the better he could see— a travois, no wheels, just a cart in triangular shape that she dragged behind her, and inside it, a child of perhaps three or four, an oddly pointed knitted cap on his head, his eyes wheeling about wildly in the viewing of nothing—he didn't seem to notice Paul or the driver or the car, though the old woman at least recognized their presence by walking a bit further to the right as she dragged her burden behind her—the child spitting as he chanted to himself, some mixture of looniness and local melody.

Paul shouldn't have scolded himself, but he did, thinking, why the hell do you have to do this to yourself, every time you see a child in some sort of distress, thinking back to your own lost babe?

But this wouldn't be my child. My child, my daughter—there he said the word to himself—would have grown up healthy and normal, whatever normal means these days.

Yes. He sucked in the smoke and held it in his lungs. And he wondered if their child had lived if he might have chosen another line of work, one that would have allowed him more time at home. Gina, with her museum job, certainly could have found a way to stay at home. If the girl had lived, well, then she would have been there with him most of her childhood, wouldn't she?

What if? He exhaled, and then immediately sucked in another cloud of smoke. What if we had been able to have another? I might have changed professions. To what? Who knows? The venture capital firm that Holden always wanted me to join, that would have been a possibility. My kind of engineering has a lot of possibilities. He puffed out the smoke and laughed out loud. Drill a hole and see the world. Yes.

"Sir?"

The driver told him the tire was ready. He took one last look around. The woman had towed the child in the cart out of his line of vision, not that he could see all that well in the dark. It was the medication he was taking. The painkiller for the ache in his hip. A climb up a high walkway over a drilling site last year in Turkey, and a simple slip, a fall of only about three feet onto a platform below, landing on his side. The pain had stayed with him.

A man takes his hard knocks, he told himself, and then climbed back into the car. Within an hour he was seated on the airplane, and in another few minutes he was flying through the dark sky, returning to Moscow—and ready for another day of meetings.

That was when he last called her, after the long day in Moscow. So many things had changed and he wanted to tell her about them, things she'd be interested in, the new clothing, the look on the faces in the crowd, showrooms for western automobiles, restaurants and fax machines and Xerox machines and cellular telephones. The shock you once felt when arriving here after leaving the West behind, well, it had turned into another kind of shock. He had wanted to talk about it. But she had been so down. The medical problem, the menopause problem, was weighing on her so heavily that he didn't really have a chance to talk about anything else.

He climbed into bed that night feeling a tinge of regret—and a fiery pain in his right hip that kept him turning from side to side. Finally, he had to get up and take another painkiller. Ah, these chemicals! He couldn't decide what was worse, knowing exactly what they did to you or knowing nothing except that they brought you some relief. He lay there a while, waiting for the stuff to take effect—hoping it would work the way it was supposed to. You are free of pain for several days, and after the first day you may wonder where it has gone, but after the second you forget about it, and another day or so goes by and you feel so normal that you don't compare your days to the bad ones.

And then the pain returns.

And you lie here like this, wondering, hoping, sometimes, after a sleepless hour or two when you decide that you will break your standard oath about taking pills to help you sleep, except that you didn't bring that particular medication along with you, stupidly, stupidly didn't bring it....

That's when he might have begun to have had some real sympathy about her troubles, all of the complaints she had brought forward—the flashes of heat and sudden shifts to cold, the sleeplessness until dawn and then the deep sleep for an hour or so, and then waking up to another day of fatigue. The strange fluctuations of desire.

Not that he didn't always try to understand. He loved her deeply and never wanted to see her in even a moment's discomfort or pain. It's just that he didn't understand the relentlessness of her unfolding condition. And she drew back from telling him the whole truth, that it was close to those years of desperate grief that they had felt after the death of the baby. It wouldn't have done her any good, she decided, to make him feel that again simply as a way to get him to understand. She loved him deeply. She didn't want him to have to feel the same pain that she was feeling.

Though, yes, of course, he understood. Understood in his bones. Or in his balls, he should have said.

The falling off of desire had been so precipitous for her that he—he had told her this once in a dark fit of desperation after returning from two weeks in Pakistan—could only compare it to a kind of death.

"Yes," she had told him. "That's it, that's just the way it is."

"But—well," he said. "The cock dies. But the cock always gets resurrected. Erection, resurrection, almost the same word, isn't it? Death in life, that sort of thing…"

She laughed weakly. Even a month or two ago she would have found him, and his word-play, amusing. Now, it was just, well, no better word for it—it just went limp. Yes, she was the one with the potency problem. She explained this to him. How all her joy seemed to have dried up in her.

"Like a black and white movie, where before all the movies were in color."

"That's going backward," he said. "What's next? You stop talking? And after that, just stills of you, not even the illusion of movement?"

"It could be, Paul," she said. "The way I feel, anything could happen."

To his credit, he did seem to understand. Or at least he tried.

"Now that I think of it, it's not all bad. After the stills, you go back to seeing the world as paintings, impressionist paintings. And then you go back to the Renaissance…"

"And eventually back to the cave?"

"Right. You'll become as stylized as one of those animals on the cave wall at Lascaux. Pure outline and shape. And magical. Aren't they supposed to be magical drawings? Paintings? Whatever they are."

She had to admit he knew how to get to her. She cooked one of his favorite meals that night, roasted a game hen, with potatoes and leeks, and they split a bottle of good red they had picked up on a brief vacation in northern California—he had carted several bottles all the way home from there, all the more to savor the wine when they drank it. That was the kind of man he was. He'd rather do it that way than go to the wine store and pick out some reasonably similar alternative. For an engineer, not bad. Yes? That was how he often put it to her. For an engineer.

And after dinner, they talked a bit more, watched the news on CNN.

"Oh, Jesus," he said with a moan when the weather report came on. "What do you know?" he said to the image of the weatherman. "You're in your stupid bunker of a studio. What do you know what it's like out there in the field?"

"You're raving again," she said, enjoying his familiar antics in front of the television screen. He was a technology *whiz, a master, but he professed to despise most of the ways it was used.*

A feeling rushed through her. All of a sudden, to use her own way of explaining things, the world seemed to be in color again.

He noticed the change, could see it in her face, a certain fullness to it, not a flush but almost. And as they passed each other while undressing for bed she touched him with a tenderness that she had been unable to muster for over a week.

So after all the talk about her retreat into her new condition, he noticed that she felt moved again, in the old way, and after reading for a few minutes he pressed close to her and asked if she would like him to turn out the light. She was perusing a handbook on organic gardening. Out near her old, long unused kiln, that would be a good place to put in a small garden. She said that to him. He asked again about the light.

"Oh, sure," she said.

Gentleman that he was, he believed in behaving this way toward all women, not just Gina, and though he often wondered, to himself and sometimes aloud, if this were all just some kind of romantic fantasy he acquired from reading certain books as a boy—because, Lord knows, in Rhode Island, where he grew up, there wasn't much of a great cavalier tradition, was there?—it was an easeful, and easy, way of getting along, particularly with women. In the dark, he was thinking about this, thinking those little thoughts that you have about your life just as you're sinking toward sleep, a little of this, some of that, a few questions that had to do with nothing, utterly trivial stuff, errands, fleeting image of something he once saw on the street in Tehran— now why would that come to mind all of a sudden?—plans for his trip east next week....

And she touched him.

"Gina, I thought—?"

"Hush," she said.

Oh, life of contradictions and complexity! Oh, depths of desire and the soaring of birds in air, fish that swim beneath the waves—but where else do they swim? They leap above the waves, some of them do, dolphins and flying fish, any others?

He awoke in the night to find her legs entwined around him, and he lay still, so that finally the sound of his breathing subsided almost to nothing and he could listen to her slight even sounds the way a mother might watch over a small child in the night, sorting out the various musics in its breathing. For a few weeks, he had listened to their own child breathing with such difficulty, first in the crib, and then back in the pediatric ward. Recalling all this turned the pleasure of lovemaking to something that tasted sour in his throat. A few hours went by and she awoke, waking him.

"What?" he said.

"I'm so hot," she said, throwing off the covers, sighing, as if nothing had happened between them.

So, yes, he understood a little of what she was going through. Of what—a dim phrase from his university days, from a philosophy course, came to mind—she was carrying with her wherever she went. Words of a French woman, philosopher or theologian, some such thing, who whenever she met someone would ask, 'What are you carrying?' Was that it? What are you carrying? What is troubling you, eating away at you? The presumption in that initial question, the assumption that everyone, everywhere, all the time, was bearing some awful pain…He understood. Or tried to. That falling off from desire that troubled her, he was sorry for that. But he wanted to assure her in a way that would not make her think that he was any less in love with her—because he was not—

that it didn't matter so much. Perhaps he himself was ⸻ a change?

Back in bed after taking that second tablet, h⸻ ⸻ trying to reason out all of the elements of their situation. That was just the kind of mind he had. But it was not the right time. He already felt close to exhaustion. And he had a long day ahead of him, and only then, after those meetings, would he fly back east, to Tashkent. And then make the drive into the Kara Kum. At least there would be a driver for that part of the journey.

So no worries, really, about that. Just this annoyance in his hip and a corresponding ache in his mind which, as he drifted toward sleep seemed to grow and then fade, grow and fade.

He floated off, and then came back again, hoisted up from below the surface of sleep by the uncomfortable burning sensation where his hip met the mattress. There was just something. Something he was carrying. Couldn't even explain it to himself. Just the falling off. Never admit it to her. But he understood. She was retreating from desire, though not from love. And he felt the same way. Which was good. Coincidence. So no uneven factors in this equation. She, me. Feeling the same, or at least something similar. Or not feeling it. So that once having put this desire behind us, like the cocoon or chrysalis of our earlier stage, we might love each other fiercely in another form?

Up early, noises in the hallway, and after his shower from the window he looked down onto streets already clogged with traffic. He wanted to call her, to tell her something of what he had figured out in the night. But he had to hurry off to the first of his meetings, and then another. By lunch, he had already turned his mind toward the flight to Tashkent. It was an opulent meal, presided over by that same portly Russian, once an official, now an executive, in the company offices. Soup, two meat courses, a roasted bird, cheeses, sweet cakes and pies for dessert.

He shook his head at the sight of it. So much had changed in less than a decade. Imagine what he might see yet within his lifetime!

Yes, Paul said, quite amazing. Miraculous.

But he had his mind on the trip, and calling her.

He had just spoken with her. So why call again so soon? He wanted to call her. Why should he need an excuse or a reason?

The heavy meal stayed with him through the afternoon. He dozed in the taxi on the way to the airport.

Goodbye, Moscow, he said to the city, feeling quite strange after he did so. He would be back in a week. So why goodbye? So long, he said to himself. I should say only, so long.

So long.

Settling in his seat in the airplane, he felt as though he might be able to sleep. But as soon as they took off he found himself unable to comfortably close his eyes. So he worked, dozing on and off, for the next six hours. I'll call her when I get to the airport, he told himself. But with all the time zones between them, what time would that be for her? He was too tired to figure it. Closed his eyes. Opened them again to find the flight attendant, trim and attractive in her dark uniform sweater and skirt, standing at his shoulder.

"Sir, something to drink?" she said.

Olive skin, oval eyes, slight squint when she smiled.

Where was she from? he wondered. Giving her his order. She smiled, her teeth were gray. Watching her move away to the row ahead. Noticing her slender olive legs, slightly bowed. Some childhood vitamin deficiency, he decided. Overall, though, she was quite pretty. And here he was, having decided the night before that desire had ended, desiring her.

He slept a little toward what turned out to be the last hour of the flight, and felt so awful when he awoke that he decided a lit-

tle sleep was worse than no sleep at all. That didn't turn out to be right. It would have been better, much, much better, if he had slept the entire flight.

Because his driver, tall, thin, with almond eyes, leaning against the side of the car and smoking a cigarette, was drunk. So Paul ordered him into the back seat and with a sigh and a big heart of regret took the wheel himself.

Sun going down. Heading west into the hazy slanting rays of light. To the south the jagged, snow-capped profile of the Hindu Kush rising as if out of a dream. Behind him the steppes—last lights of Tashkent glimmering in the rear view mirror.

And the driver slumped over to one side in the back seat.

How lovely it would be to catch some sleep himself!

But the plant lay ahead, a hundred plus kilometers into the Kara Kum.

Winds coming up, swirling dust alongside the patchy road. Good cars, these Mercedes, but the best suspension system in the world is eventually going to go to hell from riding these roads. There goes the sun. Darkness falling upon the desert with the swiftness of a lighting cue in a stage play—whoomp! All black. Took a minute for him to adjust, where suddenly he went from seeing the narrow strip of paving snaking out ahead of the car away along toward some point in infinity—though he knew that if he kept driving he would eventually reach the great cotton growing fields around Urgench on the other side of the desert—and suddenly having the world reduced to the roadway within the limits of the headlamps.

"Mr. Morgan?" The driver stirred in the back seat.

"Yes?"

"You want me to drive now?"

"I'll keep the wheel for a while," he said. "If I get too tired, I'll tell you."

But the truth was that he was already so monstrously tired that he didn't want to stop the car, but wanted desperately to keep going. This was probably hallucinatory, to think that he shouldn't stop because that would cost them their momentum, but he wasn't thinking much by now but rather was just beginning to play those games we play when we're behind the wheel and our very blood seems to turn into a sleeping potion, urging us with every pulse of our hearts to rest for a moment and close our eyes.

He sang under his breath: Mairzy doats and dozy doats and liddle lamzy divey, a kiddley divey too, wooden shoe? A song one of his aunts sang to him in childhood. And then he spelled it out for himself, for the sleeping driver, for the desert all around him. Mares eat oats and does eat oats, and little lambs eat ivy…A kid'll eat ivy, too, wouldn't you?

After that he recited a joke or two. The one about the old man the cop found weeping on the park bench…Why did that one come to mind? Who knew? And the one about the American who dies and finds himself at the gates to Hell, and sees a US entrance with no one waiting there and a Russian entrance with a long line in front of it…Old joke left over from the old regime…He had laughed at it, though, at one of those dinners in Moscow…So far away now in time, the old days, and this new life come upon them, and he thought of distances, and the distance between him and Gina…all those miles, kilometers, how many was it in kilometers? And time zones? He tried to count the time zones but gave up after a moment, trying to focus on a small flickering light on the horizon.

A fire? A signal fire? A village in flames? A burning bush?

A few minutes went by—he was still singing to himself and then singing aloud…

Softly, as in a morning sunrise…

Old jazz tune. He had loved jazz, ever since he was a kid. A kiddley divey...

And the light, the fire? Disappeared...

He found himself, the car to which he was joined at the foot and the hands, slowing down...a kiddley divey too, wooden shoe?

The light appeared again, wavering but ever-present now, and a little larger, as if the fire were floating on the darkness, and the darkness, ocean of night, desert become ocean, pushing it along on strong currents...Becoming cold, desert night, he turned the heat up a tad, thinking, give it a minute, then shut it off because don't want to warm up too much because too sleepy...

He opened his eyes, feeling the car swerve ever so slightly to the right, and it wouldn't have strayed off the road if the road hadn't been so narrow, but now—spicy juice of adrenaline shooting through his limbs—he was awake and on top of it again. Just that instant. But got to watch it...

Watch the light, the fire light fluttering in the dark.

"Mr. Morgan?"

The driver sat up and leaned forward.

"I'm all right," Paul said. "Just sit back, relax. Well, what the hell, you're probably so relaxed already you don't know what to do."

The driver lighted up a cigarette.

For a moment, all seemed well in hand, the car, the road, the dark, the fire in the distance, the smoke rising in the rear of the car...

The light disappeared once more, and Paul gave the car more juice, feeling himself straining forward at the eyeballs, as though he could somehow see through the dark all the way to their destination. And then he let his foot go a little, and the car slowed down, and he hitched up his shoulders, settled in the seat, took a deep breath, tasted that bitter smoke, thinking to himself, all right,

I admit it, I'm beat now, a little while longer and I'll pull over and let the bastard drive.

The light reappeared, closer this time, and wavering less. Watching it dance along ahead of them, how far he just couldn't tell. Minutes went by. Or seemed so. Minutes. The light ahead. This desert carries light, conducts it like electricity. Distance...Gina, yes, he must have been thinking of her...So many time zones away...He slowed down, speeded up, one more thought of her, her difficult time, so far away, wanting her close, wanting her, then closed his eyes for a second...

And awoke one last time to feel the light explode.

3.

The shock, the remorse, the sleeplessness, the discomfort she was feeling even before all this happened—it's never a good time suffering all this no matter where you are, but she arrived in Tashkent in the midst of a freak cold wave, and that seemed to make things worse. As soon as she stepped off the airplane, her limbs tingled, trembled, the chills came on.

"Last evening," Mohammed Kirov said, "the wind arrived from the north. Quite unusual for this time of year." He was a short man, with pale blue eyes that contrasted sharply with his olive skin.

"What happens now?" she said.

"You are tired?" he said.

She stood there, trembling so hard that it must have been difficult for him to see her nod.

He drove her to the hotel—another company car, since the other one was completely demolished; in fact, they hadn't even retrieved it from the desert road but had abandoned it in the small village some ten kilometers further along where Paul's body had been taken by the local official in charge of such things before they transported it, just this morning, to the morgue here in the city.

"It is much easier now than before," Kirov said, "because there is an American Embassy. I have spoken to them several times already. A man will help you. He will come to the hotel in the morning."

"Help me?" Gina said.

"With…the body," Kirov said, looking at her briefly with those eyes, and then turning away, almost as if he were ashamed. "I will be here to help as well, if you have need of me."

"Thank you, Mr. Kirov," Gina said, shivering. "I may need you. My husband made a request…"

Gina had a terrible night, worse than her worst pre-menopausal tortures back home, waking every hour, trembling with what must have been a slight fever, feeling the dark close in around her as though she were the one in a coffin—but then he didn't want to lie in a coffin, did he?—remembering what he said, remembering him.

I love my life, but after it's over, there's nothing. That's what I believe in my bones. So what's the use of burying me some-where. You love me? She told him how much. *Then I'll always be with you, you won't need some hole in the ground where my bones are buried to remember me. Will you? No, she wouldn't,* she had said.

Gina had not thought about this since the time, it must have been ten years ago, when one night Paul looked up from his desk and told her that he had made a will and wanted her to know what was in it.

"This is standard," he said.

"I don't want to talk about it," she said. "I know it's completely irrational, but that's the way I am. I didn't like to touch pictures of insects in books when I was a child. And I don't want to talk about this."

"You at least ought to hear about how I want to be taken care of."

"Taken care of?"

"When I die."

"You're not going to die in the near future," she said. "We'll worry about it when it happens."

"Just listen to you," Paul said with a laugh.

"I know," she said. "I can't help it."

But before the next few minutes had gone by, he had cajoled her—that was the charm he had had over her ever since they first met—into agreeing that she would have him cremated.

"Cremated?"

Bruce Goldstein, the consular official who met with her the next morning, gave her a very odd look as he repeated the word.

"Yes," Gina said, staring at him across the desk. "That's what he wanted."

Goldstein, young enough and serious enough so that this might have been his first foreign service post, shook his head.

Gina leaned across the table where the remains of his breakfast lay—she had no appetite at all but had ordered a pot of tea just to appear sociable—hoping this boy would take pity on her. Despite all of the torment of her sleepless night and the constant ache that she now felt on the left side of her chest, she still retained some small amount of rationality. And this prompted her to wonder if he looked at her in this way not because she was a problem that had been dumped in his lap but simply because of how she thought she must appear to him. Haggard, dried up, worn by grief to a zombie-like state in which she moved along with her duties, head bowed, still trembling a little from that fever which might have come on her with the current cold wave.

"Will you help me with this, please?"

Goldstein squinted at her from behind his small, wire-framed eyeglasses.

"I will, but it's not going to be easy. This is a Muslim country now. Well, it always was Muslim, but the Soviets put a chill on the religion. But since independence…"

She crumpled then, sitting there in the nearly empty restaurant, indifferent waiters standing at some distance—why did she notice such things in moments like this? who knew?—and suddenly feeling all the air go out of her, her arms jerking awkwardly across the table, knocking cups and cutlery aside, her head sinking down so that her forehead touched the place setting.

"Mrs. Morgan?"

Goldstein came around to her side of the table.

"Are you all right?"

Her limbs trembled—that same chill, something she ate, something she breathed, or the wind from the north blowing down across the tundra and taiga, high desert and mountain, or all of this together to make a terrible force against her—ice in her throat and breasts—her head aching so hard that she feared her skull might burst open—and in her thighs a throbbing emptiness, something she had felt only once before, when she had delivered a dead infant.

"Please," she said, suddenly following an urge to stand up.

"Of course," Goldstein said, putting his arms around her.

"You'll help me?"

"Yes, I will," he said.

So odd—she could feel him hard against her.

"You promise?" she said as she pulled away. Her hands went to her hair, to her face.

"Yes," he said, lowering his eyes in an embarrassed way.

"Thank you," she said, snatching up the napkin and touching it to her eyes.

He excused himself, giving her his card and saying that he would call as soon as he could. She folded the card over once, twice, four times on her way up to her room. Then she lay down on the bed and tried to sleep.

Just like Paul, as she had imagined him. Beaten down by time and travel, so exhausted that there was nothing that could help him except perhaps pills which he always refused to take. But then he was taking the medication for the pain in his hip. The doctor had warned him. No driving at night. She jumped up from the bed, filled with anger. Didn't he know better! How could he have done this to himself! Done this to *her!*

She reached for the telephone and began a call home. It was—what?—nine time zones earlier, or ten? Or was it ten time zones ahead? When the call went through, it rang and rang. Finally, an answering machine.

"Hello, you have reached the office of Dr. Betsy Cohen—"

She hung up, took some deep breaths and reached the operator again, trying another number. So much easier to call now, Paul had told her, because all the calls didn't have to be funneled through the state apparatus where they could be monitored.

I don't know who would want to listen in to this call, Gina said to herself, unless they had an interest in misery.

"Janice?"

"Hello?" Her sister, at the distant end of the line, sounded as though she had just come in the door of her apartment. Gina couldn't remember what time it was there. She remembered her sister through a haze—she hadn't spoken to her in months.

"I'm in Tashkent," Gina told her, and began to explain why.

"No, no, no!" her sister screamed. *"Oh, Gina, I'm so sorry! Are you all right?"*

"Do I sound all right?"

"No, you don't. You sound awful."

"It's the connection, Jan," she said. "Believe me, I'm holding on. I have business here to do."

"Business, what business?"

Gina told her about Paul's request.

"I didn't know he wanted that," her sister said.

Her voice suddenly faded, replaced by crackling static.

"That's what he wants," Gina said, continuing to speak as if her sister were right there in the room. Or inside her head. "Or wanted. God, to say that in the past tense! It's so awful. You change a tense, he's dead, not, I mean, because you changed the tense, but just such a simple thing in language, and it means so much! We never talked about it. Why would we talk about it? No reason. You don't think about these things. Except at some point he must have. And decided what he wanted. He wasn't a very religious person…Oh, there's that *fucking* past tense again! Oh, Jan!"

Her sister, not usually so sympathetic, this time lent her her ear.

"I should be telling you that I have to hang up, that I have all of this business to take care of here, Jan, but I don't want to hang up. I want to hear your voice."

"I'm flying out," her sister said.

"Don't be silly," Gina said. "I'll finish this business today. And be gone by the time you get here. It's a long flight. Over many time zones. I can't even begin to think about why they have so many damned time zones here, and we have so few."

"Do your business," Jan said. *"But I want you to call me tonight. Promise? No matter what time. Okay?"*

"Okay."

"And go to the embassy. There's an embassy, isn't there? They can help you."

Gina pictured young Bruce Goldstein, the strangeness of his hard cock against her when they embraced. For the inexperienced, a first experience.

"They're helping," she said. "They're sympathetic."

"They better be," her sister said. *"That's their job."*

Gina took a deep breath.

"And on top of all this…."

"What is it?" her sister said.

"I feel so strange."

"Your husband…Oh, honey, please…do you have any thing with you? Some kind of medication?"

"Paul took his medication," Gina said. "The jerk! The bastard! The fool!"

Silence.

"What? Gina, I'm losing you at this end."

"I have to go," Gina said. "I will call you."

Another try at a call to Dr. Betsy Cohen, this time to her home number. They were friends more often than they were doctor and patient, but these past few weeks, the way she had been feeling, it reassured her that her pal knew medicine. But what could medicine know?

"You have reached the telephone of—"

Gina cut off the call and sat back down on the bed. She noticed that her breath was coming up short and punchy. Remembering some exercise from a yoga class she had taken years before, she tried to calm herself by regulating her breath. *In-take slow, ex-hale slow-er...In-take slow, ex-hale slow-er...*Maybe it was beginning to work. The day was growing brighter outside the window. She closed her eyes against it, lay back against the pillows. *In-take slow, ex-hale slow-er...*She pictured her father's body in the funeral home about ten years before, his face rendered alien by the embalming process. He had raised her to think of a place after death called Heaven. Seeing him there in his casket so shocked her that it did away with whatever residual hope she might have clung to about an afterlife. He looked like a zombie in a midnight horror show.

But not so fast, girl, she could hear her father say. That's just the body. What about the spirit? All your college education, did it kill the spirit in you? This body is just the container for the spirit, he said. You drink the water, not the glass. A phrase out of a literature course came to mind, whose source she couldn't quite recall. Wouldn't it be pretty to think so? Hemingway, yes, it was Hemingway. Papa, he liked to be called.

Papa, she said, is there a heaven? And if there is, will you talk to Paul now, Daddy? she said to him in her mind. You're together now, if there is someplace to be together. But if there were, why cremation? Could she take a chance? But then if there were a heaven, he wouldn't need the body. Not if Daddy was right. The water, not the glass.

She sat up, thinking she heard a noise. Then fell back onto the bed again. She felt almost as if she had been poisoned. Her throat dry, her stomach aching, her head aching. She began to weep, and then cough, and then cry again. After a while her crying subsided and she lay there, as still as she could make herself, listening to the sounds of the foreign room.

It was so bizarre when she awoke to the beeping of the telephone, knowing immediately what had happened. Six months without a period and now, suddenly, she was bleeding.

"Hello?"

She stood there, shivering, clutching a fistful of cloth in one hand and pressing it against her crotch, staring out the window at the treetops, the white sky beyond.

"Mrs. Morgan, I think I've found a way," said Bruce Goldstein, his voice so faint and the line so full of static that he might have been calling from America rather than the embassy here in the city.

"The logistics are rather complicated," he said when he met her in the lobby. The place had been nearly empty when Gina had met with him before. Now it was full of men, many of them in nicely tailored European suits. A banner across the front of the room announced in French an international conference on Boyle's Law. Whatever that was. Goldstein held out a sheaf of papers, and ushered her to a relatively quiet corner of the room. "A lot of paper to sign."

Gina put her signature on whatever he showed her.

"So," he said, "we're on our way."

She looked at him.

"Please," she said in a voice that she did not recognize as her own. "Would you please? My husband's dead. It's not a school picnic."

"Sorry," Goldstein said. "I didn't mean to be disrespectful. I've only just started here, Mrs. Morgan. I know the language, but I don't really know my way around yet."

She might have said something then, but chose instead to pick up the papers and hand them to him.

"I'm ready."

But she wasn't. Something strange and awful happened to her when they left the hotel. Outside the air was warm. The cold wave had passed almost as if it had never been. But five minutes into their ride, her body began to clench up, and she was sure that her impromptu method for stanching her new flow wasn't going to be sufficient—who could have predicted? Although Dr. Betsy Cohen had said she couldn't call it menopause until twelve months without a flow. And this was only five months. Or was it six? And it was one day with Paul dead. She began to cry.

Bruce Goldstein slowed the car down and pulled over to the curb.

"Are you all right?"

Men in robes walked past, stared at them. Veiled women carrying small children like packages at their hips followed along behind the men.

"No," she said. "Would you be all right?"

"No," he said.

"Where are you from?" she said, trying to calm herself. *In-take, ex-hale. In-take, ex-hale...*

"New Jersey," he said.

"Paul was from Rhode Island," she said.

"Yes, I know," he said.

Gina said nothing.

"I'm not a spy," Goldstein said. "I looked him up in *Who's Who.*"

"He was well-known in his field," she said, recalling the entry. *Paul Morgan, born…* She started crying again.

"Mrs. Morgan?"

"Drive," she said through her tears. "Just drive."

Block after block of new apartments gone to seed. It was growing hot in the car and Gina rolled her window down, enjoying the odors of the streets. Diesel fuel. Sweet rotting garbage, even that. And then they crossed into a more modern part of the town, and arrived at a drab grey building, clearly official in some way.

"This could be difficult, Mrs. Morgan," Goldstein said as he led her inside.

"It's all difficult from now on," Gina said. "Since yesterday. Or whenever it was that man called me."

"Kirov? Mohammed Kirov?"

"Yes, Paul's company man out here. He met my plane. I'll see him for dinner tonight. If I'm up to it." She shook her head, shivering again.

"He explained to you how it happened?"

They were walking down a long corridor that smelled of chemicals and cleaning fluid. Gina found the astringent odors rather pleasant, considering the circumstances.

"He told me," she said. "It wasn't much different from the way I imagined it. Paul was exhausted. He fell asleep behind the wheel."

"There was a driver," Goldstein said.

"Paul took the wheel. He liked to take charge. They were going to some desert town."

Goldstein said the name.

"That's the one," Gina said. "It was late. He was tired. He shouldn't have been driving at night. He was on medication. But he liked to take charge."

They had kept on walking and now they stopped in front of a set of doors.

"Here?" she said.

"Yes," Goldstein said.

"I don't know if I can," she said.

"I'll be here with you," Goldstein said, but he didn't sound very sure of himself.

Gina shook her head.

"Is this a hospital?"

"It's the city morgue," Goldstein said.

"Do they have a pharmacy here?"

"It's just the morgue, as far as I know. As I told you, Mrs. Morgan, I haven't been here long."

"But you speak the language?"

"I speak Russian, and I speak Uzbeki."

"When we're through here, can you find me a pharmacy?"

"Sure," he said.

"Why are you looking at me like that?" she said.

"I'm not," Goldstein said. "I'm trying to help, Mrs. Morgan."

"Then let's go in," she said, pushing against the door.

There's no even rhythm to life after something like this, Gina decided. Not after she walked in, saw the morgue workers in their white coats, went directly over to the table where several of them were standing. Goldstein, coming up behind her, said something to the people in white. They said something back to him. They rolled up a table on wheels. One of them said some-thing to Gina, the man pulled back the sheet, and she fainted.

If he hadn't made that flight to Alma Ata and back. If he hadn't been so tired because of that. If he hadn't been taking that stuff for his hip. If the driver had not been drinking. What if the driver had still been drinking but Paul had not been so tired? What if the driver had still been drunk but Paul had not been taking his medication for the pain in his hip? What if the truck driver roaring out of the desert had not been roaring? All these *ifs*…and even now, as she was opening her eyes, feeling Goldstein's hands helping her to her feet, she was living through a dozen new *ifs,* a thousand of them, a million, ten million, each one of her cells an *if* in itself. And what *if?* What *if?*

"I hope you're feeling better," Goldstein said.

"Let's just get it over with," Gina said.

They were driving through the city, followed by a van carrying the body.

(The body! Gina said the word over and over to her-self. The body, the body, the body, the body. Paul's body, Paul? Not Paul. Paul was gone. Paul lived only in her memory and in her heart. So he was alive for her, but to himself, gone, no longer here, dead, his body, body, body, body. The body.)

A haze hung lightly over this part of the city as Goldstein drove them past cement block buildings, brown trees, pavements occupied by groups of families, mothers swathed in wraps, body-gowns, hoods, veils, the men in shirts untucked into their trouser waists, jackets, male children in sweatshirts—*Harvard,* she noticed on one, *Santa Cruz* on another, *Nike* on another. She pointed these out to Goldstein.

"If they have such a love for the West, why can't they understand cremation?"

"Muslims don't cremate, remember?" he said.

She didn't like this manner of his, or his voice, a mix of guttural New Jersey and whatever fancy private university he had attended.

"Just as bad as the Christians," Gina said.

"And the Jews, too," Goldstein added. "They—we—don't cremate either."

"Well, I guess I know where my new allegiance lies," Gina said. "Did it take a lot of doing?"

"Like I told you, I'm fairly new here, Mrs. Morgan. But I've developed a few contacts."

"Next time it will be easier," Gina said.

"What do you mean?"

"Next time you have to arrange a cremation."

"It's not something you want to be ready for," he said. "Mr. Morgan—"

He didn't actually pause, but whatever he said as he went on speaking, it made Gina's heart feel as though it stopped, and everything seemed to spin around her, the inside of the car, the light outside, the streets.

She lost control.

"You creep! Don't talk about Paul that way, do you hear? Don't talk about him as if you knew him!" Deep, awful sobs rasped out of her, and she rocked back and forth in the passenger seat.

"Forgive me," Goldstein was saying while this was happening to her. "Please, Mrs. Morgan, I know you're upset, I'm doing my best for you, I'm doing all I can…"

After a while her sobbing ceased, and she began to feel sorry for him. Not such a callow fellow. Forgive him? At least he knew what to ask for. But he must be cold-blooded by nature, which is what this kind of job he did—was it a profession?—seemed to require. She could picture him at Princeton, or wherever it was that he went to school, smug, superior, expecting that people would come to him. She wondered if by now, after only a short time in the world, he had begun to understand how often he would have to go to people for help.

She watched his face as he drove, so impassive, his eyes studying the street.

"Do you know what to expect?" she said.

"I've never seen this ceremony," he said. "When I was in India—"

"You've been to India?"

"Not to work. I was still at Princeton—"

"Ah," she said.

"What?"

"Nothing. Go on."

"You're feeling a little better?"

"As well as can be expected," Gina said. "Go on. Tell me what you know about it."

"Well, it's a purifier, fire is for them. I've sat through six-hour food purification ceremonies, where they bless the food stuff to be eaten in a new dwelling."

"A dwelling."

"You understand what I'm talking about. It's an old way of life. They don't have houses, they have dwellings."

He looked over at her, almost as if he expected her to smile at his wit.

But she refused him the smile, although, if she were being truthful with herself, she did feel a slight urge to smile.

"Tell me more," she said.

And so he told her the rest of what he knew and by that time she had grown calm, resigned, and they had reached their destination, somewhere on the eastern edge of the city, on streets hedged in by mountains behind them. It rather amazed her how quickly her emotions changed. From low to high, high to low. She wanted to talk to Dr. Betsy Cohen about this. She wanted to talk to someone who might be able to explain.

So here they were, driving up in front of a compound of several low white buildings set around a large courtyard, one of which appeared to be a temple of some sort. The young black-bearded men in robes who met them at the entrance reminded her of people she had seen in photographs in books about India. But books are one thing, reality is another. She wasn't prepared for the sound of their sweet, low baritone voices. For the lucent rich darkness of their beards. Or for the powerful scent of incense that surrounded them wherever they walked.

"Sorry, madam," one of them said.

"Thank you," Gina said.

The van had pulled up behind their car and the other two men were helping the driver and his assistant lift the body out of the back.

The body. Swathed in white.

The men struggled with their burden, carrying it into the compound.

"Come," said the man who had spoken to her. "You will sit with us while they prepare the body."

Gina, feeling as though she were in some sort of dream, followed along, bathed in the stream of incense he left behind. She had once been to Mass with a boyfriend at college. She had been to a Jewish wedding. She had been to a Greek wedding. But Gina was a woman raised in perfectly plain Protestant earnestness by parents who believed in nothing except heaven and all these events, even the Mass, seemed much too festive for her to count them as religion.

"What have I gotten myself into?" she said to Goldstein as they walked through the courtyard to the temple building.

A low monotonous chanting had begun inside.

"This is what he wanted, isn't it?"

"He wasn't a Hindu, he wasn't anything," Gina said, shocked at the coldness in her voice. Was she so exhausted now that her spirit had gone flat? Maybe this was the way Paul had felt, worn out, washed out, when he climbed behind the wheel of the car and headed into the desert after dark.

Inside, a half dozen more bearded men, some with hair as white as pure silk. And women swathed in colorful cloths of red and gold and white and blue. Everyone sat on the floor, gazing up at a low platform where a young man with smooth dark skin and a long black beard chanted before a small flame, every now and then looking up and out over the crowd. There was something about his eyes.

The monotonous chanting continued, a constant whirring now in her head.

A young boy came up to her and said, "Shoes, please, madam."

Gina looked down at his bare brown toes and immediately slipped out of her shoes. She noticed only then that Goldstein had removed his shoes before they stepped inside.

The chanting rumbled on.

Gina looked around, noticed a beautiful gold and red mandala just above the place where the young man chanted above the flame. And a statue of a man with four arms and the head of an elephant off to one side in a niche above the front of the room.

"An elephant god," she said.

"Ganesh," Goldstein said, as though he had grown up in the religion.

"They're praying to an elephant god," Gina said.

The chanting increased in volume, though the rhythm remained steady, the noise all vowels almost, a pleasing sound, noise she could live with. The rhythm, the rhythm: *I said you could have some food, today…I said you could have some food, today…I said you could have some food, today…* Over and over and over. Gina eventually settled onto a cushion on the floor, Goldstein sinking down alongside her.

"My…people," he said, "they prayed something like this…back in ancient Jersey…"

She found herself smiling at his joke, and then losing herself once again in the vowels of the chant.

I said you could have some food, today…I said you could have some food, today….

Odors arose from the bowls of smoky incense at the feet of the man on the altar. Gina fixed her eyes on the elephant god, the snaky trunk, the headdress. The smoke wound its way toward a mandala carved into the ceiling. Sound swelled, vowels increased, smoke bent in the light. What must have been an hour went by, and then, as if on signal, the man at the altar turned to look at her with eyes that seemed to whirl in his head.

Yes? she asked him with her own eyes, suddenly obsessed with the notion that they could communicate in this fashion.

You are the one? he said with his eyes so fiercely crossed that Gina expected that sparks might fly from them at any second.

Yes, I am.

You are eye?

Gina felt her body begin to tremble. She stood up, but found herself too weak to do anything but immediately sit down again.

Eye am sorry.

Eye am, she said.

And he was yours?

We were together.

And he has gone?

Yes, I think, she said.

But he will return, he said.

Return?

Paul, dear Paul, goes back to the whirl from whence he came.

But don't you believe in reincarnation? Where to then? And will he be himself?

Eye don't know, who can say? But he will come back, whether as cricket or leafy palm or a drop of rain or a sunset, one way or another. Thus it is, always.

Everyone rose, and Gina discovered that with a little effort she could stand with them and then walk with them—they moved purposefully, though not at all in a hurry—outside to the courtyard. Atop a wooden platform surrounded with neatly arranged firewood, Paul's body—it had to be Paul's body, yes?—lay swathed in white, covered with flowers, the feet pointed toward the south.

A gong sounded behind her and bells tinkled. Gina turned to find the young man with the wild eyes at her elbow. The perfume of his hair and the spices he exhaled nearly bent her at the knees.

"Please, to begin," he said. "And Mr. Stingold? He will be in the assisting of you?"

Gina nodded, recovering from the shock of finding herself so close to him. His head, his hands, his arms, seemed to give off great heat—she stepped back from him, feeling dizzy again. More bonging of gongs, more bells. Beneath the blue-white cupola of sky, a cloud of incense floated over them. Women in saris sat before the platform, breathing in unison, holding up their hands and making their fingers into signs, ornament-like, that Gina thought they might cast as shadows onto some screen not yet visible.

"Mr. Stingold?" Gina said as Goldstein came up alongside her. She felt the beginnings of a smile on her lips—unheard of! As quickly as it began, she erased it. "What happens next?"

"The priest or swami or leader, whatever he is, he's going to show me," Goldstein said. "I have a few things I'm supposed to do in this. They won't let you, even though you're the wife. Until the end."

"Some other time I might fight about this," Gina said. "Right now, I don't care. Just do what you have to do."

The man with the dancing dark eyes returned to her from wherever he had been.

"Now, please, Missus, you are sitting here."

He gestured toward a set of pillows directly in front of the platform. Gina sat, while Goldstein ducked close to her ear and said, "He's been telling me the mantra."

"The what?"

"What they're singing," Goldstein said.

"Tell me," Gina said.

"Something about letting your eye go to the sun and your life to the wind, the you being the deceased, your husband…Go to heaven and then to earth again…reincarnation, you know?"

"I know," Gina said, feeling almost as though she might actually know, even though she did not.

"Or you are going to the water," said the dancing-eyed man as he kneeled down in front of Gina. "He can be going anywhere, depending on his living in the past."

"He was a good man," Gina said, feeling her throat tighten.

"Then after his journey up to heaven, he will be going then to be returning to a better place."

Better than me? Better than with me?

Gina felt a surge of heat in her chest. Dr. Betsy Cohen, where are you when I need you? And what would you say, seeing me praying to an elephant god? And burning my husband's body?

"And now," said the swami, "we begin with the fire wherefrom he came here, wherefrom he was born…"

Two women moved through the crowd, holding wooden bowls before them. People reached into the bowls. When it was Gina's turn, she saw that the containers were filled with cooked rice steeped in milk.

"You are taking some," the woman said to her, "and throwing half away."

Gina plucked a sticky wet ball of rice from the bowl and, under the woman's steady scrutiny, touched her lips to the mass before tossing it onto the ground.

"And now to your husband," the woman said, urging Gina forward to the platform where with the woman's guidance she took another ball of milk-soaked rice from the bowl and this time loosened the grains and sprinkled them before her.

Up close, the body, wrapped in swaddling, had a fragrance of its own, and not at all offensive, smelling of incense and something similar to sweet butter. Paul had had a hardier odor, less sweet than rough, something that always reminded her of wood and tree-bark, of rocks baked in the sun. The memory of it nearly made her swoon again, and Gina stepped back from the platform, bumping right into Goldstein.

"Are you ready for this?" he said.

"What do I do now?" Gina said.

"Follow me," he said. "Not that I know what I'm doing. I'm just following him."

They walked around the platform three times slowly, led by the dark dancing-eyed man and accompanied by the now almost abrasive sound of the chanting.

"What are they saying?" Gina called to Goldstein over the droning of the devout.

"I don't know," Goldstein said, "but as I told you it's not entirely unfamiliar to me."

"I think I'm on another planet," Gina said, smiling at the man with the lively eyes as he approached them after their third time around the platform.

Gina felt the breath rush out of her when she saw the smoking torch in his hand.

"We say these things," the man said, holding up the torch. Gina inhaled the hot raw air around it. "Mr. Stingold would supposed to be saying, but I am saying it for him this time. Now I am applying fire to all the limbs of this person, who willingly or unwillingly might have committed lapses in this life and is now under the clutching of death, this person being someone attended with virtue and vice, greed, and ignorance. But in spite of all these flaws, very human imperfections if I must add these words myself, we are hoping he is to be attaining the shining regions up above…"

He held out the torch.

"Here then for you, Mr. Stingold."

"I'll do it," Gina said.

"The wife," said Goldstein.

The dancing-eyed man stepped back.

"Most important is the fire, rather than the person who ignites it."

Gina stared at the torch, the harsh odor of tar and fire rushing fiercely into her nose.

"Would you like me to do it?" Goldstein held out a hand.

Gina shook her head.

"Mr. Stingold," said the dancing-eyed man, "it is better for the wife."

"Better?" Gina stared at the smoky torch, breathing hard. The fumes both repulsed and attracted her, but at this distance she couldn't escape them.

"Better than not," the man said.

"I don't know if I can," Gina said.

Goldstein stepped up to her.

"Really," he said, "I'll be happy—"

"Get away!" she said to him in a nasty voice she scarcely recognized as her own. Turning to the dancing-eyed man, she said, "I'll do it."

"Very good," the man said, handing her the torch. "Touch the fire now to this place." He pointed to a make-shift wick made of rags at the base of the platform.

Gina's hand trembled as she ignited the pyre, and it took a moment before she could tear her eyes away from the flames and gaze up at the white cocoon at the top of the wooden mound.

Paul? she said. Paul?

She heard nothing. She felt nothing but a certain light-headedness.

Flames exploded at her feet and she danced away from the platform.

"Oh, Missus!" the dancing-eyed man cried out as he leaped toward her and began beating on her skirt.

"Jesus," Goldstein said, "you're on fire!" He too began flailing at her skirt.

Gina stared in amazement at her smoldering hem as the dancing-eyed man led her to a place on the ground some distance back from the now blazing pyre.

Suddenly she felt an enormous thirst. As if they could read her mind, several women approached her with bowls of rice and milk, and water.

"Can I drink the water?" she said to Goldstein as he sat down beside her.

"I wouldn't," he said.

"Maybe we should go now," Gina said, staring over at the small conflagration atop the platform.

"We're supposed to wait until sunset," Goldstein said.

"I guess we'll wait then," Gina said. She felt so odd, chilled again, despite her proximity to the flames and the smoky odor of her clothing. And then, after a few minutes, feverish again. Maybe I should climb up there and go with him, she was saying to herself. But she knew it was too late for that, even if she were crazy enough to try.

"And there is the matter of the cow," Goldstein said.

"The cow?"

"We're supposed to pay them with a cow. The soul of the departed, your husband's soul, rides it to the next world."

Gina said nothing, watching the flames flutter against the darkening eastern sky. She felt heat in her heart, but her head and limbs felt cold, nearly numb.

"But they'll take dollars instead," Goldstein said. There was a catch to his voice as if he were trying to somehow lighten things up. What a fool! But Gina instantly forgave him, she felt so sorry for herself.

The two of them sat there as the flames flickered and settled. Had that much time gone by? Gina was beginning to get hungry and hating herself for it. She looked over at Goldstein, who was pretending to be so grim and sympathetic. After a while she said, "What do I do about the ashes? Aren't I supposed to do something with them? I've never thought about such things. One day Paul and I are talking on the telephone and the next, I'm watching his body consumed by flames. And I'm asking myself why I am not completely overcome, seeing what's happening. And then I tell myself, it's because I'm dead, too—"

"No, please, Mrs. Morgan, don't—" He reached for her.

She pulled away.

"Oh, stop! Let me talk! About the ashes. I don't know. I suppose I should, shouldn't I? What do they usually do with them?"

"They scatter them in the sacred Ganges," Goldstein said, looking rather perplexed, hands at his sides, head lowered slightly. "But I don't know about here. There's no sacred river. I'll ask them, if you like."

"No, no, don't. I'll take them. I'll scatter them myself when I get home. Though I don't know where. Paul and I only talked about this once. You never expect this to happen, even if you've talked about it. I don't know where to scatter them. Or should I keep them? I just don't know. I don't know." She took a deep breath, inhaling the odor of smoke, and listening, over the sound of renewed chanting, to the crack and snap and bark of the lively flames.

4.

"Hello?"

"Hello."

"Oh, I am so glad that I caught you. All these time zones…"

"Gina?"

"Yes, it's me."

"Where are you? I had those messages…My God, I'm so sorry…"

"Thank you, thank you. I know. It's…beyond terrible. I'm…I don't know. I can hardly talk. But I need to talk. Do you have time?"

"I have time. Are you still there in…?"

"I'm in Rome," Gina said. "Don't ask me why. I don't know. I was coming back from Uzbekistan…"

"Are you sure you're all right?"

"Do I sound strange? I'm not surprised. I've seen some very strange things these past two days. Paul…his body…the flames…"

"You had him cremated?"

"That's what he wanted. And In Tashkent, it's mostly Muslim. They don't cremate. We had to find Hindus."

"Was that difficult?"

"I had help from the embassy. A man named Goldstein. The swami was very funny. He called him Stingold."

"The swami?"

"One of the Hindus. He led us in the ceremony. Three times around the pyre…I should have jumped on it myself. As it was, I caught my dress on fire."

"Bad?"

"Not bad enough."

"No, no, no, Gina…"

"Oh, don't worry. I'm alive, but only barely," Gina said. "Oh, God, Betsy, it's so comical, it's grotesque. I was taking a urine sample for those tests when I got the telephone call. But I don't need to take any tests anymore. I don't need to think about taking hormones, do I? And on top of it all, I had a period. What is the point of it? Can you tell me?"

"Oh, my God. Gina, oh, it's all so…"

"Absurd? I've thought of that. But what do I do now? I don't know what to do now." A pause at the other end of the line. Here she was, on long, long distance, staring at her suitcase on the floor in the far corner of the room. A small package, containing the sealed jar, lay within, under her underwear. Gina began to count. One, one thousand. Two, one thousand. Three, one thousand. Betsy Cohen spoke again.

"How long will you stay in Rome?"

"I wish I knew. I told you, I don't know why I came here. I just saw the flight posted at the Frankfurt airport while I was waiting for my plane home. I remember saying to myself, you can go anywhere now. Without Paul you can go anywhere, you can do anything. It's a bizarre feeling. I hope you never feel it. It's not that I was a prisoner of our life together or anything like that. You know that. You know I was happy with him."

"Uh-huh…"

"But now that's over. And I'm free. Almost like I'm the one who's ridden the cow into the next realm, not Paul."

"The cow? You'd better explain that to me. I'm not sure I understand."

"Oh, I'll talk to you about it when I get back, so much you'll want to throw up."

"No, I'll listen. I want to hear."

"That's part of your job, isn't it? Meanwhile, what do I do?"

"What do you do? In Rome?"

"In my life."

"Gina, come home and we'll talk. It's much too early in this for you to have any answers. It's all still too fresh."

"I'll try to get a flight back tomorrow," Gina said. "I really don't know why I'm here, anyway."

"Let me know what you decide."

"I will."

"And Gina?"

"Yes?"

"We still should run those tests."

She was terribly hungry and had some food sent up to the room, a sandwich, prosciutto, olives, a beer. It tasted so delicious she wished she had ordered another one. She could, she could. But she was so tired that she got quickly undressed and climbed into bed and turned out the light.

What time was it?

Only ten in the evening when she awoke suddenly and sat up in the dark room, trying to remember where she was.

She got out of bed and used the bathroom. Her bleeding had stopped, almost as if it had never been. Yet she still felt that same odd feeling that she had felt for weeks and weeks, logy, weak, tired but not sleepy, bloated and yet hungry. So strange, she thought as she climbed into the shower. While the hot water pounded on her back, she was content. But then she had to turn the water off and do something other than stand there dripping before the steamy bathroom mirror. She cleared a space in the glass and stared at herself. Dark circles under her eyes, matching almost the dark nipples of her sloping breasts. She turned to one side, then the other. What a thing to think about! She hated herself. But her hair needed cutting.

Gina got dressed and took the elevator to the main floor. The lobby was quiet, with noises filtering out from the bar. Voices. Music. She went straight to the front door and stepped out onto the street. The night was warm, the air a lovely mix of smoke and perfume. I would ride an elephant here, she said to herself, but then I already am here. In the distance, a claxon sounded. Across the street a group of teenagers walked along, smoking, laughing, girls holding hands with girls. A pair of men—on the prowl?—strolled along behind them, just far enough back so that you could tell that the two groups were not together. Which one am I rooting for? Gina sighed, unsure as to why, except that it was not fatigue, and stepped back inside the hotel lobby.

A man passed her on his way out—dark-haired, broad-shouldered. She hadn't been looking, she barely caught a glimpse of his face. Was he wearing eyeglasses? At the bar, she looked at the men, beginning with the elderly barman, polishing glasses. He was kind, he understood that she was going through something. He brought her a Campari and soda. After that she asked for champagne. After a second glass, she allowed herself to think about what she feared to think about—the flaming pyre, the walk around it, the way her dress had smoldered.

When she looked up from her bubbling drink, she noticed that at least three men were staring at her. Two of them instantly looked away. She toyed with a stirrer, a dried lemon rind, a book of matches someone had left on the bar. One more swallow of champagne, she told herself. One more only.

Back in the room, she is lying naked on top of the covers, feeling a little tipsy, her eyes fixed on the jar that she has placed on the night table next to the bed, when someone knocks on the door.

Yes?

A man's voice on the other side.

What?

Need to see you, he says in a strange rough accent.

Just a moment, she says, and gets up and goes to the other side of the room and digs in her bag for her nightgown and pulls it on.

Yes? She opens the door a crack and peers out at him.

It is a man, eyeglasses, dark hair.

I could not help but think of you, he says.

I…can't hear you very well. You have such a thick accent, she says. You'd better come in.

Only for moment, he says as she opens the door. (She's thinking, why do I give him a Russian or some kind of Slavic accent? What do I want with that?)

He's slightly taller than her, thick neck, but a tender smile. From those eyes you can tell that he has suffered himself, lost loved ones, perhaps in some terrible invasion of his hometown.

She grasps his hands—they don't feel as rough as they look—and pulls him down to her on the bed.

You don't have to explain, she says.

Thank you, he says. In your eyes I see the same.

Do you?

I do.

It's so hard to talk about, she says. You say something simple, like, My husband has died, and yet there is so much complication behind those words.

I had a wife, the man says, his breath warm on her face.

Is she...?

She is gone, he says. Along with my children. Three daughters.

A war? In a war?

He sighs, and she feels herself roll toward him.

Life is a war, he says, and takes her in his arms.

From this point on, things go quickly, and it is difficult for her to slow them down as he pulls her nightgown over her head. Almost as though she were assuming a posture in that yoga class she took years ago when Paul first began his long travels, she opens her legs to him in a wide vee.

The bearded man she met years ago in the Moscow zoo, though aged not at all, kneels before her on the bed, dips his head toward her.

Please, she says, you must be kind to me.

With a woman like you, he says, I can be no other way.

His lips meet her lips, his tongue works at her like a wild mollusk loosed from its shell.

Oh, my God, she says, writhing beneath him. I feel it? Do you feel it? Oh, it's so...I can't say. Oh, God, oh, oh, oh...

And she looks up to see Goldstein, his shirt undone, his chin tucked up, his thin chest almost devoid of hair, leading a large brindled cow into the room.

You, she says, where did you come from?

He shrugs, and turns to the cow as if to ask it this question while the cow lets flop a huge stinking pot of dung onto the rug.

And only then does she notice the elephant trunk waving over her, tracing out some mystical symmetry in air.

Ganesh, my Ganesh, she says in a whisper.

Eye am here, he says. But his voice is different, almost as if he were speaking over a telephone on a long-distance connection…

Oh, she says in a little moan as the slender naked Hindu hops on top of her, smiling, laughing at her with his dancing darting eyes before the undulant trunk swaying between his legs begins to probe her.

Oh, my God, the pain! The friction! Terrible singeing heat! The smell of burning hair, coppery stink of burning blood…

clothes burning

sheets on fire

volumes of smoke and heat rising all around her as the bed is consumed and she floats on the flame as though it were a boiling yellow-hot sea…

pubic hair and lips hissing flesh navel searing along with her buttocks bubbling with hot puckering fat her stomach wrenched open by fire intestines cooking now her breasts oh each breast roasted and fire traveling quickly up her throat to her face, skin pulled back by the flames as though fire were a surgeon and eyes pop in the heat and her head next, last, the end…

her spirit tears loose from her charred and smoking body resting on its bed of flames in a room consumed with smoke

her spirit ready now to mount the flatulent cow and ride...

Oh, Ganesh...

Suddenly she feels Paul's spirit hovering next to her, his soul arisen from the ashes and spinning vortex-like in air...

I'm sorry, she says to him, and even before she can explain, about the man with the eyeglasses, the man at the zoo, about the dancing-eyed swami, he motions in her mind for her to hush...

We're together now, he says, speaking in rhythms she never knew he was capable of while alive, *all else behind us, and that is what matters...*

Darling, my love, she says in a way that she never could seem to conjure when they were alive together on earth...

Oh, yes, here we go traveling, traveling to the light...

Light, yes light...

—Morning comes, as she awakens, throat raw, eyes sore, head throbbing, to the remainder of her days.

THE EXORCISM

1—The Couple in the Next Room

The first people I want to forgive are the couple—or at least the woman of the pair—in the room next to mine in the quaint old hotel where I always stayed when I came up to attend to my daughter at college. This time was not really a visit, since Ceely—that's my daughter—was going to have to leave school, and after a long day's drive to fetch her about all we had time for on the evening I arrived was dinner at a pretentious and over-priced Italian restaurant that always gave me hope when I spent time in this college town and always dashed my hope to the floor.

Ceely went back to her dorm for one last night, and I went to the hotel. It had not been a good day, but then it had not been a good year. For starters, Ceely's mother, Billie Benjamin, whom I also forgive, my first wife, and one of the country's best female jazz pianists, after a sudden illness as they say—in her case, a hot-shot of heroin administered by a much-younger musician boyfriend—had died. Ceely had been nearly inconsolable ever since. And my present wife, of whom I had always said since I met her would be my last, had not taken well to the funk I'd fallen into at the news. Though I forgive her for this.

"It's not like, you know, I hadn't put all those years behind me," I said to her during the middle of a terrific argu-

ment about whether or not I would go to the funeral (well, cremation ceremony, actually). "You were never jealous when
Billie was alive, but you are now that she's dead?"

"I lied," she said. "I've always been jealous."

"Because you think I've secretly been in love with her?"

"You don't live all those years with somebody and then
just toss the feelings down the drain," she said. "But that's not
why I'm jealous."

"Oh, not this, not now," I said, really in distress.

I always seem to marry talented women, and my second
wife, Charmaine Rosenthal (I always seem to marry talented
Jewish women), whom I also forgive, is no exception. Her problem is that she is talented in so many ways that she never could
settle on those one or two things that she could focus all her energy on. She had been a successful CPA when we first met, over my
tax return, and soon after we married she decided she wanted to
give up that practice in order to raise poodles, which she did for a
few years (and from which time we still have our little Bela
Barbark, a white poodle with all of the charm of a newborn and
the brains of a monkey, whom I decidedly forgive for all of the soft
little turds she leaves behind on the dining room floor). From the
dog stuff, she went on to start a mail-order business in medicinal
herbs (which is how I eventually came to meet you, Erna), and tir-
ing of that she opened a small boutique in Georgetown,
bankrolled by a couple of her richest female friends—I forgive
them all—who loved her taste in clothes (and each of whom
owned a poodle bred by Charmaine at the kennel on the edge of
our former property in Oakton, just south of the Potomac).

But for all of her gifts—and it did seem as though she
had a magic touch in whatever business she found herself in—
Charmaine still was not happy.

"I haven't found myself," was the familiar refrain I'd often hear around the dinner table, with the little tag at the end, "the way you have."

The thing is, and I have said this to her a thousand times, I was one of the lucky ones, or so I thought, who was never lost.

My late father, whom I also forgive, owned a wholesale electrical supply business, and from that I developed my hobby of listening to music, and at college, our little gem of a state university right here in the northeast, I studied acoustical engineering, and then started building, and then—quite a different thing—designing, sound systems for a living. (Billie and I met because of that, when I was testing the sound board at a concert she was playing at our local arena—Jersey Jazz! Listen to the Stars!—and we clicked from the beginning.) I had met a lot of musicians, because of my work, and I'd even slept with one or two (well, maybe just one, a thin blonde violinist for a visiting orchestra, with an outsized talent for oral sex—she should have played a wind instrument, and I forgive her for taking up a stringed instrument instead—whom, for a number of reasons, I've never forgotten). But with Billie, there was more than just a click, there was a bang, a crash, a thunderclap!

"Man," she said to me in the middle of the night after her concert, "I may be just a kid but I've gigged around a lot and I've got to tell you that I've never felt this great before!"

Billie, so cool a stylist that a small industry of critics has flourished trying to get to the icy heart of her work, and in bed, at least with me back then, she was a buttercup, a reed in the wind, a lost little girl.

How to explain her origins! Her father was a philosophy professor at the New School of Social Research in New York City and her mother a well-known criminal defense lawyer. Billie went to the Dalton School and grew up in the whiter-than-white section of Park Avenue (except for the Jews like her own family). Maybe it was the criminal part of her mother's work that spoke to her, because as soon as she could hum a tune she was singing, and as soon as she was singing she was scat-singing, and as soon as she was scat-singing she was transforming an expensive education in classical piano into a darting, fly-by-night, hit and fade away jazz style that took everyone by surprise. Professor Hans Epstein, and Joanna Epstein, Esq., I forgive them both. (Though they have been so formal in their communications with me since Billie's death that I almost shouldn't.)

So, Erna, here we are at the ceremony, Ceely all busted up, and Charmaine pissed off, and though I understood completely Billie's final wishes for the cremation (which consisted of some Bud Powell and then some Monk and then some Bill Evans playing over the badly maintained loudspeaker while her body was rolled into the flames) it didn't give any of us much room for what is so fashionably these days called "closure."

Ceely went back to school, I returned to a project that included constructing the sound system for a major new West Coast concert hall, and Charmaine, who had never closed her doors, kept on selling to the fashion-deprived of northwest Washington.

Things simmered down. Or seemed to.

Until about a month later when I was standing at the window of my Seattle hotel room enjoying the silence after a day of sound, sound, and more sound, staring mindlessly at the monumental slopes of Mount Ranier as they caught the slanting rays of the departing sun, and someone knocked at my door.

Well, not just someone. It was the blonde violinist.

"What are you doing here?" I said, just that brusquely. Not a hello. Not a how surprised I am to see you, and pleased, after all these years.

Just—"What are you doing here?"

My brusqueness didn't faze her at all.

"I'm the concertmaster and I asked about the sound."

Well, she made sounds, I made sounds, and given what I know about the acoustics of these modern high-rise hotels, I worried that we might be doing some damage to the sleep of others. I didn't think much about the damage I was doing to myself.

A week later, I arrived home, my work completed, and my bags full of remorse. There was a note on the dining room table saying that the dean of Ceely's college had called—yes, I forgive her—and asked to speak to me at once.

"She didn't say why?" I was a bit agitated when Charmaine got home and I asked about her conversation with the dean.

"I told her I was the wicked step-mother," Charmaine said, "and that she could tell me everything. She chose not to."

"Because you inspired such confidence," I said.

"Have you called Ceely?"

"I've tried a bunch of times. I'll try again." So I went to my desk and punched out her number.

And got "Blues in F," Billie's famous tune. With Joshua Redman on saxophone, and I can't remember the names of the drummer or bass player. Ever since she bought an answering machine, Ceely changed the music just about every day from one of her mother's recordings to another. I'd heard this one enough today to be able to name all the chord changes, the whole progression.

The tune. Then, "Hey, this is Ceely, leave a message…" Pause. Then the tone.

"Me again," I said. "Phone home."

It wasn't a good night. I lay in the dark, the weight of the slender violinist full on my chest, and Charmaine becoming more and more pissed by the minute.

"She's done something awful, I know, I just know. The way the dean spoke to me, even the way she breathed…"

"Maybe," I said (with hindsight, rather prophetically), "she just has a distinctive voice. Sound is my business, right? I'll let you know when I speak to her."

I run my own business, I can take time off whenever I like, though in practice this means I put in much more time than if I worked for someone else. But this next morning I got up early, went to the gym, and did an hour on the treadmill while listening to the middle part of a long crappy novel about American Plains Indians by some dreamy-minded former anthropologist. At this hour of the day I worked out with a bunch of hard-charging Washington lawyers, (one of whom I saw there regularly, and since he was the husband of one of Charmaine's pals, someone who spoke to me in the locker room, usually remarking about whatever it was his wife had recently purchased at Charmaine's shop). This time it was a designer shirt that showed her nipples through the fragile material.

"Do I want my wife walking around showing her nipples?" he said as he jammed himself into his suit trousers and prepared to get ready to argue some intellectual property case that had to do with a logo for a bakery chain (as he told me in between comments about his wife's nipples). "She's a little too old for that," he said, and then he paused, and added, with a candidness quite uncommon for Washington, "She nursed four of our kids with those nipples, and now she wants to show them off all over town…?"

I felt responsible somehow for his distress, but I forgive him for making me feel that way.

He left the locker room looking as though he could step right onto the stage of *Inherit the Wind* and debate William Jennings Bryan while I went into the shower, trying to remember his wife, and her nipples. I struck out. Charmaine's I remembered, having seen them only the night before when she got undressed for bed, roseate half-dollars. Billie's I remembered, having been going over and over in my mind since her death (a not uncommon thing, right?) everything I knew about her—they stood out on her small chest about the size of an infant's thumbs. Ceely I hadn't seen naked since she was an infant, and I invoked the Incest Taboo so I wouldn't have to wonder about her. But I was almost immediately distracted, anyway, as I was leaving the gym and passing me in the doorway, on her way to her own early morning workout—and I don't know her but I forgive her—was a compact little woman in designer sweatpants and halter top with nipples so taut and distended they pressed against the inside of the material of her sports bra and halter with the intensity of tiny wild beasts yearning to be free.

Well, forgive me for that, but I'm not a poet, just a sound engineer trying to make sense out of things.

At least that's what I said to myself on the way home.

Where Charmaine was getting ready to leave for the store, and basically ignoring me. It was almost the hour when I could call the dean and so I poured myself a cup of coffee and picked up the newspaper and when another half hour had passed, picked up the telephone and made the call.

The dean—already forgiven—in an as yet unremarkable Middle-Atlantic voice told me Ceely had gotten drunk and broken into the college concert hall and set the baby grand piano on fire.

It was still fairly early in the morning, but I suddenly felt much too fatigued to explain this act to her, and so mumbled something about driving up at once so that we could have a conference. The dean said that she would be happy to speak to me, but that Ceely had already been given an indefinite suspension.

Just as I was hanging up the telephone, Charmaine was going out the door. And so I didn't have a chance to tell her that I was leaving. I tried Ceely's number again. More "Blues in F." I left a message that I was driving up to see her and then went upstairs and packed a small bag, grabbed some books and tapes and CDs, and left the house. Within a few minutes I was moving slowly along in rush hour traffic on the Beltway, in the first stage of my journey north, angry at all these other drivers—but forgiving them now—because they impeded me in my trip the way they did.

Fortunately, I had brought those tapes along. A month or so before, I had finished listening to the latest Tom Clancy novel and had just bought the newest Stephen King, for listening to on my headphones while running the treadmill. Why this junk (which I forgive both Clancy and King for writing)? I've never really thought about it until now, but maybe it's because I listen to so much good music while doing my job that I need to kind of clear my head when I'm trying to relax. If exercising is relaxing. I don't know.

I had stopped in at our local bookstore café one morning the week before to grab a coffee on the way back from the gym and wandered around looking at the shelves where I usually found the junk I listened to. There was some good stuff there that I already owned, some mysteries by Tony Hillerman and Sara Paretsky, an abridgement of *Huckleberry Finn* read by Paul Newman (I forgive him for reading an abridgement), and some stories of his own read by Barry Lopez (no one I need to forgive) with background music by the cellist Paul Winter (him either). That's where I found it.

A new translation of the *Bhagavad Gita* (not that I had ever listened to, let alone read, the old one), by a guy (whom I don't need to forgive, either) named Mitchell. Why I bought this I can't really say. It just seemed like the right thing to do at the time. Maybe it was the weird title. In our family we'd hardly ever gone to church, and I'd never read much of our own Bible, so in an objective way it seemed pretty stupid that I had my hand on this CD of the Hindu holy scripture. But a lot was happening even then before I knew it, and I was just following along.

So here I was, the traffic beginning to move a bit once I got on I-95 in the Baltimore direction, on the very trip for which I had bought that spiritual CD, without even knowing it at the time. But first, there was Billie. I kept a supply of her stuff in my glove compartment, and one of the first discs I pulled out of the holder was "Billie Plays Monk," from that incredible series ("Billie Plays Basie," "Billie Plays Ellington," "Billie Plays Mingus," "Billie Plays Miles") that culminated with the posthumously released "Billie Plays Billie," one of the all-time best-selling albums in the modern jazz repertoire. Holding the disc in front of me, glancing down at the photograph that made her look so gamine-like and vulnerable, I could hear her saying, "Not bad, for a lame white bitch, hey?"

All the way past Baltimore and on toward New Jersey, I listened to her out-Monking Monk. Hours later, I was still listening to her while skimming across the George Washington

Bridge and driving into the upper reaches of New York City, emerging from the wreckage of the Bronx on either side of the road as though from a dream I scarcely remembered.

Billie, I said to her in my mind, what did I know of you and what did you know of me?

It wasn't until I crossed the border into Connecticut that I thought of slipping in the Hindu disc. Normally, as I said, I would have put on some of the usual crap, the Clancy or the King or one of their second-tier imitators like Harold whateeverhisname or Dean Koontz. But I had run out of that junk, and was left with the prospect of silence, or more Billie (and by that time I was, I have to admit, Billied-out), or the *Bhagavad Gita.*

I probably should have chosen the silence, since because of my work, as I might have mentioned, it was often that state that I desired most. But instead, as if some larger hand were guiding me, I chose the *Gita.*

If you don't know that story, and since you grew up in the Judeo-Christian tradition you may not, it's easy enough to outline it to you. This hero named Arjuna is driven in a chariot onto a battlefield in a war between his clan and another and when he reaches the no-man's land between the two armies he refuses to fight. At which point his chariot driver (who is God in disguise) begins to speak to him about life and death and everything in between.

Good things to listen to while you're driving through Connecticut, which seems like a strange mix of country green and strip-mall white.

> *I am the taste in water,*
> *the light in the moon and sun,*
> *the sacred syllable Om*
> *in the Vedas, the sound in the air...*

Om, I said to myself as I rode along. Om…, remembering it, I think, from some Allen Ginsberg concert I had helped stage at Rutgers many years before.

> *I am the fragrance in the earth,*
> *the manliness in men, the brilliance*
> *in fire, the life in the living,*
> *and the abstinence in ascetics…*

"Om," I was saying now quite loud, "Ooooommmm…"

A little further along, as I was turning north onto Interstate 93, God said,

> *Because most men are deluded*
> *by the states of being, they cannot*
> *recognize me, who am*
> *above these, supreme, eternal…*

"Om," I said. "Ooooommmm…"

God said:

> *I permeate all the universe*
> *in my unmanifest form.*
> *All beings exist within me,*
> *yet I am so inconceivably*
> *vast, so beyond existence,*
> *that though they are brought forth*
> *and sustained by my limitless power,*
> *I am not confined within them…*

"Om," I said, enjoying the sound no end, "Ooooommmmmmm…"

By that time I was approaching the little green Massachusetts college town where Ceely, still in the steel grip of grief, had set fire to a baby grand piano.

It was late afternoon when I checked into the hotel and was given what the young woman at the desk assured me was the last available room. I called Ceely's number and listened to a fragment of Billie's tune "Jew-Bop," whose title, when the album with the tune first appeared, had nearly started a war in the pages of the *New York Times* arts section. I left a message and then lay back on the bed. I was hungry, really hungry, but I didn't want to miss Ceely's call so I decided to close my eyes and stay put a while.

I dreamed a little, but I won't go into them here, since, like most dreams, they were fairly confusing and inconsequential and by the time I awoke to the ringing of the telephone I couldn't remember much of them anyway.

"Hello?" I said.

"Father." (That's what she called me, like something out of an English drawing room, and I've never understood why, but I forgive her.)

"Honey, honey, about time," I said, and told her I would meet her at her dorm in fifteen minutes.

I am the vital fire
in the bellies of all men...

The CD started up when I turned on the car and left the hotel parking lot. I turned it off and drove through the little town toward the campus. Students roamed the streets, as if looking for something that might put their wandering souls to rest. It was early evening, early spring, and I was hungry, and I was going to rescue my only child, and I had buried her mother (well, you know, she was cremated, etc.), my own parents had been dead almost a decade now but suddenly right there in the downtown street I missed them both terribly, and I was mostly indifferent to my wife's nipples, and I had to pee— I should have peed before I left the room—and I didn't know what I wanted to do with the rest of my life.

When I arrived, my daughter was pacing up and down on the porch of the student house where a few other young women sat smoking or leaning on the railings, while a bulky mahogany-skinned young fellow in a blue coat and cap appeared to be standing guard. As soon as she saw me, Ceely gave a toss of her beautiful long blonde hair and flicked her cigarette over the railing and came striding toward me wearing what I thought at first was one white glove.

I am not an extremely tall man, and Billie was by anybody's standards pretty much of a half-pint—until she sat down at the piano stool or, to be honest, when she climbed into bed in a romantic mood—so how we produced this tall blonde string-bean of a daughter I can't figure without putting sound aside for a while and taking up the study of genetics. Here she was, sleek and sylph-like, opening the car door and sliding gracefully onto the seat.

"Father, this is Rashid," she said, and it was only then that I realized that the bulky guy in blue denim had followed her to the car. When he leaned in to speak to me I saw that the cap that I had figured for part of a security guard's uniform bore the inscription "Jumping Jack Flash" (and I forgive Rashid for that). Scrolling out from beneath the cap were tight dark curls and he had an appealing half-smile on his face that allowed me to see his sparkling but somewhat crooked white teeth.

"Mr. Swanson," he said, sticking out his hand across Ceely's chest.

"Hi," I said, shaking his hand briefly and then letting go. The faint odor of gasoline hovered in the enclosed air.

"He saved my ass," Ceely said (so much for the English drawing room). "Or my arm, anyway," she added, holding out her bandaged hand. "Rashid got me to the infirmary right away."

That's how the three of us came to be seated in that Italian restaurant, the two of them talking me through Ceely's story while I wolfed down a large plate of thin spaghetti and tomato sauce and large chunks of bread and a salad. They had eaten, they could talk. And I let them, feeling both pleased and annoyed that it wasn't just Ceely and me, because she and I had grown quite distant ever since her mother and I had divorced (when she was three) and the distance had been compounded in an incalculable way by her mother's death. And while dinner for just the two of us would have been a rare opportunity for us to talk, a particularly important opportunity, I had to admit, since she had just committed that outrage here at school, I figured that we would have more than plenty of time on the drive home, and that Rashid deserved some reward for assisting her in her hour of need.

It became pretty clear that he was almost a hero. He was the one who followed her to the music hall when she had the gas can in hand, and he was the one who tried to wrestle it away from her, spilling gas all over his best new baggy jeans and hiking boots. And he was the one who, after she managed to splash the fluid across the top of the piano and flicked on a borrowed cigarette lighter and ignited the stuff, pulled her back from the flames and rushed her to the infirmary with her third-degree burns. (Though there was something about him that I didn't like, something I just couldn't put my finger on.)

"My God," I said, "she could have burnt herself alive."

"Father," Ceely said, sipping the soda she had reluctantly ordered since she was not yet old enough to drink, "that was what I wanted to do."

I listened in astonishment as she explained how she had planned the event, first going to the local Wal-Mart and buying a gasoline can, and then walking to the nearest gas station to fill the can, as if she had just run out of fuel up the road, and then meeting Rashid, who helped her to sneak in to the concert hall.

"How could you have done this?" I said as much to him as to her. I knew how she could have, she was so despondent about her mother's death. But him? All I had to do was look at the way he gazed at her and it was pretty clear. He worshiped her. If she had asked him to help her burn the town hall or assassinate the president, he would have willingly gone along.

I forgive him. Because as attractive as she was, it wasn't just Ceely who lured him along. It was her mother. Young black college student, smart (you could see this in his eyes almost immediately), sensitive, raised on jazz (as he told me while I was making the near-fatal mistake of drinking a second coffee at the end of the meal), madly in love in a puppy dog sort of way with Ceely (and who wouldn't be? just look at her and your heart leaps), and when he learns who her mother was, his heart goes crazy, and he's attached to her for what he views as life.

He was almost a hero in all this. Almost, because without the pot that he had supplied she never would have gotten so stoned that she would have gone ahead with her cocka-mamie plan in the first place. But there he was, right at her side, not playing the part of the voice of reason and saying, Ceely, Ceely, this is stupid, this is wrong, but rather, in his stoned innocent way, saying, Yeah, this is a tribute, girl, a way to honor her, your mother she was so cool you'll make this real hot for the bourgeois bitches at the college.

I understood the pot logic of it all. Billie and I spent our entire short marriage stoned out of our minds. Pot brought good cheer into the world, it made some punishingly straight lines waver a little, it made you laugh.

But in this case I wasn't laughing.

I got the check and paid for dinner and drove them back to Ceely's house and told her to be ready to meet me at nine the next morning. And to be packed by then and ready to leave. It was a long drive home and I wanted to get started on the early side.

"Home?" she said, looking at me as though the word were in a foreign language.

"Yes," I said. "Home. You're coming to stay with us for a while."

And it was only then, when the light of the street-lamp near her house reflected in a funny way in her eyes, that I realized that she was still stoned.

"See you in the morning, sir," Rashid said and then turned and led Ceely back to the house.

Women rule the world, don't you think? I mean, superficially it's run by men, but when you strip away all the crap there they are, the true law-givers and truth-makers. I was thinking that while watching Ceely walk away, thinking how mothers (unless they kill themselves with a hot-shot) keep their daughters all their lives, but men have to watch them walk away on the arms of reasonably pleasant but morally oblivious young college boys who supply them with the pot that keeps them calm while they try to burn baby grand pianos in honor of their mothers' death.

Nobody prepares a man for this, I was thinking as I returned to the hotel and got ready for bed. I was, as I mentioned at the start, fairly well exhausted.

After I had finished in the bathroom I called home.

Charmaine answered in her familiar sleep voice.

"I was dozing," she said. "So how did it go?"

I gave her a short version of the events, leaving out the stuff about my own emotions and the drugs.

"She's coming back?"

Silence.

"Char—"

"I'm here. I'm just thinking."

"What's to think?"

"Where will I put her?"

"Where she always stays, where else?"

"I mean, where will I put her in my head."

I tried to talk her through this. But it didn't do much good. We both pretended to be happy by the time we completed the call. I was not happy. But I did expect that I would have a good night's sleep.

I had forgotten about drinking that cup of coffee after dinner. That gave me the sort of buzz, the kind that goes on for a while after you turn out the lights. I lay there a while. Then I got up. I peed. I drank water. I went back to bed. And since I'm a sound man, I lay there a while and I listened to what lay beneath the silence.

The faint susurration of water in the hotel pipes. Was it hot? Was it cold? My mind had calmed to the point where this seemed like an interesting question. A line from the recording drifted into my thoughts: *"I am the taste in the water…"* The elevator cranked its way between the floors and then stopped. Its door slid open…and then clanked shut. Footsteps. Fading. The music of the pipes hushed loud again in my ear, against the faint underbeat of my pulse. In the distance beyond the hotel, suddenly a siren, wailing loud, and then fading as a police car chased some local hot-rodders.

I sighed, breathed, thought of Ceely asleep in her dorm bed only a quarter of a mile from here. Was she lying there in the arms of young Rashid? What was it about him that I didn't like? I pushed the thought away, and my mind drifted again along the shushing water pipes, the noise like drum brushes washing beneath a bass line, "Blues for F," I was thinking, Billie, her face, her nipples, Ceely's…And then I admitted to myself that I couldn't stand Rashid because he was the same age as Billie's deadly last boyfriend.

I was lying there, simmering in my hate and despair, and I must have dozed off because the next thing I remember is the slamming of a door.

Where was it? Was I dreaming? I sat up and listened, muffled sounds coming through the wall behind the head of my bed.

A woman's voice, with a man's bass rumbling beneath it.

The woman again. Water running, shifting of furniture.

I lay back, sank back into the near-silence.

I drifted off again.

And then it began.

On the other side of the wall (her voice clear, his voice muffled throughout).

Oh, Jack.

Nice.

Jack.

Very…

Jackie, honey…

Got you…

Feels so goo—

Baby…

So…

So good…

Yeah…

Baby…

—

Jack, come on…

I'm com—

Jackie, no, no…

Can't it…

More, more…

You…

Now, now…

Oh, I…

Now, yes, yes…

Hold a…

Ohhhhh.

Yeah…

Ohhhhh…

Yeah…

Ohhh…

Thumping, bumping, like animals tumbling between the walls. At first I listened with a sort of prurient sympathy, no more amazed at the noise of it all than if I had been a child awakened in the night by his parents' lovemaking. This was life in the raw, I said to myself, two people going at it in a room in the dark in an early spring New England night.

Coming…

Ohhh…

Oh…

A long time went by, and my amazement grew, not just at the fact of it, but at their stamina. They were like horses, they were like lions, and they stomped and thudded and cracked and yowled on the other side of the wall like animals in the wild.

Except that animals deplete themselves almost at once. And this was now going on for a human length of time.

Please…

Yes…

Please, please…

Yes…

I jumped out of bed and went to the window, the sounds from the other side quieting a bit if I put my ear to the glass. I could even hear the buzzing of a street lamp outside.

But I couldn't stand here all night, and eventually retreated to the bed.

To hear more of the same combat on the other side of the wall.

Oh, Jack…

Yeah, you…

Oh, Jackie…

How long, Lord? I asked. How long? Without even knowing to what god I spoke. It didn't matter to me. I didn't care. I wanted them to finish. I wanted quiet.

Ohh…

Yeah…

Oh, my God…

That's…

Yes…

Now I staggered out of bed, stood close to the wall, debating with myself about whether or not I should give it a good pounding.

No, no, I said, no, let them go on undisturbed. I felt tears running down my cheeks as I confessed to myself that nothing I had ever done in my own life had been this passionate.

(And without knowing what I was even doing, I forgave them, Jackie and his unnamed girl.)

2—The Dogs

I awoke at first light, basking in the luxurious silence that enveloped the room, the floor, the entire hotel, the street, the town, perhaps even the state and the entire eastern seaboard, the nation, the hemisphere, the world. The headache hit me just as I lay my head back onto the pillow, hoping for more sleep. I had clocked only about three hours, and I was suffering, and my compassion for the couple in the next room had evaporated in the night.

I knew my room number and from that subtracted two, and picked up the telephone and punched out that new number. Through the wall I could hear their telephone ring once, twice, and then I broke off the call. Three more times I did this before either of them could pick up the receiver. I could hear faint mumblings. I punched the number again. I got up, took a shower, and called the number again. Twice more, and then I got dressed. Twice more. And then I left the room.

The lobby was deserted, except for the young college boy behind the desk. He looked up at me as I passed by, but didn't speak. It was cool outside, and the hot coffee I found at a little doughnut shop on the main street filled me with warm cheer. After a while I returned to the hotel, called the room next to mine several more times, and by then it was almost time to meet Ceely for breakfast.

She was waiting on the porch, smoking and staring into space, in a dark sweater and baggy jeans looking beautiful and fresh, which made me, in my nearly sleepless condition, feel as bad as I had ever felt. But Rashid wasn't there, and so I sighed a father's sigh of relief.

Ceely tossed away the cigarette and picked up a bag and carried it to the car.

"What about the rest of your stuff?" I asked.

"Rashid is going to put it in the storage room for me," she said, settling into her seat.

"That's awfully nice of him," I said. "That means you plan on coming back?"

"Father," she said, as if that were an answer.

"Father," she said again when I reproved her for ducking out of the breakfast place for a quick cigarette.

"You'll have to direct me to the dean's office," I said when it got near the time for our appointment.

Silence for a while as Ceely sipped at her coffee. "I'm not going," she said.

"Hey," I said, "Charmaine is fixing up your old room—"

"I mean I'm not going to this meeting," she said. "I don't want to talk to that lame bitch. She's the one needs psychiatric care. Lonely little dyke."

I sighed and wiped my mouth with my napkin, looking around the room as if there might be something the waitress could do for me. That was when I caught a glimpse of Rashid standing outside the restaurant, leaning against a parking meter, smoking casually.

"Okay," I said, "you wait here. I'll find the dean and come back to get you."

Ceely looked a little unnerved because I wasn't applying any pressure on her to attend, and it gave me a secret pleasure to have outfoxed her even on this tiny point as I gave her a quick kiss on the cheek—she took it stoically, without blinking—and left the restaurant. Outside I asked Rashid for directions and went on my way.

This dean, again, I forgive her, was not what I expected.

Probably not even thirty, she was a lovely freckle-faced strawberry blonde dressed in a white blouse unbuttoned down to her sternum where a Star of David dangled between her rather fulsome breasts. Before she even opened her mouth, I was confused.

"You're the dean?"

"This happens to me a lot," she said, extending her hand toward me across her desk. It was surprisingly cold to the touch.

"You understand why?"

She laughed, and I felt a splash of painfully pleasant body chemicals wash up and down my chest.

"Mr. Swanson," she said.

"Tom," I said.

She cleared her throat.

"Tom," she said, and just the way she said it made her voice seem so familiar. "We all love Ceely here, you understand."

"She's very lovable," I said, wondering about where I might have heard her voice, and then letting go of the thought.

"She's suffered, that we know, too."

"She has," I said.

"Her mother was terribly gifted."

"One of the rising young stars of jazz," I said.

The dean smiled, cleared her throat again. "Not my favorite music. And rather esoteric these days, what with hip-hop and all that."

"Do you like hip-hop?" I asked her.

She unfolded her ample lips in a smile.

"Would you believe that I've written about hip-hop? My field is psychology, and I did my dissertation on the effect of hip-hop on learning-disabled inner-city children."

"That is extraordinary," I said.

"But, now, Ceely…"

"Not a learning-disabled inner city kid," I said.

"But in her own way disabled," she said.

The telephone rang. She looked at me, and I looked at her and nodded. She picked up the telephone.

"Hello?…Uh-huh. Oh…Oh…" She looked over at me, and I looked away. "Oh…"

I looked back at her.

"Oh…yes…yes…Okay…Bye…"

She looked back at me as she set the telephone on her desk. I looked over at her, wondering if I was going mad.

"Sorry."

"I'm the one who's sorry," I said, "I didn't get much sleep last night. Worrying about this, you know."

"Certainly," she said. The look she gave me made me believe she understood. "Where did you stay?"

I told her.

"Such a lovely place," she said. "A little shabby these days, but lovely. I stayed there when I first moved to town, before I found a house. Sometimes, I like to put people up there. When I have an overflow of house guests."

I cleared my throat. "I'd like you to send me a bill for the piano," I said.

"We may be covered by insurance," the dean said.

I shook my head. "I doubt it. I know a little about that sort of business, musicians willfully destroying instruments and such. Unless you have a specific clause…"

"I'll check into it," she said. "Meanwhile I don't want you to worry about it. I want you to think about Ceely."

"You've suspended her," I said.

"Pro forma," the Dean said, raising a hand to her mouth to mask a rather large yawn. "Oh, excuse me."

"Think nothing of it," I said. "Late night, huh?"

She stared at me, a tiny smile on her large attractive lips.

"A friend of mine came to town," she said. "A…a girl I went to college with."

"Oh," I said, "and you stayed out late. Where do you stay out late in this little town, anyway?"

"You're showing your big-city chauvinism," she said.

"You're the one who writes about inner-city kids and hip-hop," I said, not sure what I meant. "So where did you go?"

"You really want to know?"

"Sure," I said.

She stared at me, and stared a little more. She didn't know what was going on, I didn't know what was going on, but it was going on.

"We went roller-skating," she said.

"Roller-skating?"

"That's right."

"Isn't that amazing?" I said.

"It's just a small town diversion," she said. "A small college town diversion."

"What's your friend's name?" I said.

"What?"

"Just curious," I said.

"Mr. Swanson, I don't think my friend's name matters much in our current discussion."

"You just want to keep your personal life out of this matter, right?"

"Yes, of course. Why shouldn't it be? Mr. Swanson?"

"Of course, of course," I said. "I don't know what I was thinking. I'm pretty exhausted myself. Forgive me. Forgive me?"

The first real wave of fatigue—and there would be many that day—washed over me, and I suddenly wanted out of there. I told the dean that Ceely and I would talk on our drive home about intensifying her therapy.

"Tell her to call me if she needs to talk," the dean said. "I'll give you my home number in case she needs to call me there."

"I will," I said. "And don't forget to send me that bill."

"I'll be in touch," she said, again offering me her hand, still cold as ice.

An hour later, and Ceely and I were rolling out of town.

"What's this?" she said, turning on the CD player.

I dwell deep in the hearts
of all being; I am the source
of memory and knowledge…

"Just some stuff of mine," I said, clicking off the player.

Ceely immediately found the discs of her mother's music, and as we passed through Springfield, Billie's version of Mingus' "Better Get It In Your Soul" filled the space around us. All through Connecticut we listened.

Finally, I said, "I was hoping this drive would give us the chance to talk."

But when I glanced over at her I saw that she had fallen asleep.

Driving back through New York City, and with Billie's music still in the air, I had a lot of time to think about what I wanted to talk to her about when she awoke and to rehearse how I might phrase it.

Taking a deep breath in my mind, this was how I began: Your mother and I got married very young. This sexual spark snapped between us when we met, I know, I know, you don't think about your parents and sex, or at least you don't want to think about it because you find the subject slightly disgusting, that's really the other side of the Incest Taboo, I think, and if you don't know what that is, I'll give you the short version and if it interests you, you can take an anthropology or a psychology course when you come back next term, whichever department they teach that stuff in these days, I'm not sure, and I hope you are planning to come back next term, meanwhile, we'll find you a good doctor, and maybe you can get a part-time job, at Starbucks, maybe, or at the bookstore, Politics and Prose, you always liked going to their cafe, maybe there's a job for you there, I know the owner slightly since I go in there a lot, I could go in and speak to her. But the main thing is the therapy. You've got me very worried, Ceely, setting that piano on fire, burning your hand, you might have done yourself a lot worse harm than you did to the instrument, and I know, I know how you must feel, not just the way your mother died but the way she lived, even when you were just an infant you were separated from her because when she was home she was out gigging until the early morning, and then you would wake up and she would be asleep, and so I would pack you in that kid-holder and take you with me on jobs, Celia, Celia, I hold in my heart those first months of your life, and when she went out on the road we wouldn't see her for weeks, and I was the one who fed you the bottles and took you to the doctor and sang to you, though when she came home it was always a great little occasion, and she played for you and wrote tunes for you— "Ceely's Wail," from her second album, and that incredible ballad, one of the most beautiful pieces of music I know, "Dawn for Ceely"—let's put that on, unless it's just too difficult for you to listen to, though I know from your answering machine that you listen to her work all the time, there, oh, Lord, that melody pulsing forward, but never so fast that you miss the effect of the chords, a burst of beauty, like the nostalgia for all the days gone by that you'll never see again, and the melody picks up, filling you with such hope for the future—with your mother out on her gigs, in the city and then after the albums began to win her a national audience, out on the road, I knew exactly how you felt, thinking to myself quite a lot, you marry somebody and then you hardly ever see them they're working so hard and making such a success of what they do, you're happy for them beyond words, but regret creeps in, you begin to feel a little jealous about the other musicians who see her more than you do, and the audiences who get to see her in her best form in those mid-evening hours when her hands are warm, her fingers flying, her head zig-zagging to the rhythms of the tune, and the sound she's making out of that oblong box with strings filling your heart with such extremes of joy and despair that you wonder how you'll ever find the way back to real life. Sure, she'd be home every day she was playing in town, but she was sleeping a lot of the time we were awake, so even when she was with us she was apart, so we didn't so much as actually separate as kind of erode, like a beach washed away after one heavy tide after another. I just remember, one minute we were all out in the park on a Sunday when she was playing a Jazz Summer gig, and the next thing I'm walking past the doorman into your grandparents' building with you in the pack on my back, tears in my eyes. I'm sorry, baby, that it happened, and it wasn't anything either of us did, just a kind of natural falling off of desire and affection—but what at your age do you know about such things falling away?—so that where once we felt like one flesh and one mind we later felt like the two people we actually were, not that I recommend being realistic over being romantic, for instance your stepmother and I got married because in a rational way we told ourselves that it made a great deal of sense for us to do it, given our common interests and admiration for each other, though right now I can't remember much about what those interests were and what we admired each other for, no, no, baby, life is just much too strange and inexplicable to try and figure out, and much too straightforward in its own way—you're born, you grow up, you get old, etc.—to think about in any kind of mystical way, either, at least, that's what I used to think (absolutely that's what I used to think, until I had my session with you, Erna), most people taking one side or the other, either the romantic or the rational, and never rising up to the even more troubling, puzzling level of the paradoxical where you hold both views in your mind at once, oh, I was going to say all these things to her, but she kept on sleeping.

And so I tried to listen to more of the Gita—

In this world, there are two persons:
the transient and the eternal;
all beings are transient as bodies,
but eternal within the Self....

And with New York City now behind us, I was thinking how it was once Billie's city, the place she loved as a child, for all of its parks and museums, and a city of music, where she filled her heart and young soul with all varieties of concert performances, and then scouted the jazz clubs with fake ID when she had only just started into puberty, she told me all about this when we were getting to know each other, the way she conned the older brother of a black kid at her school to become her escort to some of the best jazz venues in the city, a business-like arrangement, a couple of feels for a concert, and she gave him money for all the cover charges and the drinks (though she didn't drink at all at the time). Lord, the night she went to Harold's and stayed around until closing, her escort zonked out at the bar, and everybody thought she was the daughter or the niece of the owner Mr. Primack, so when as the last set ended, and the drummer was packing up and all of the patrons were leaving or had left, she hopped up onto the stage, just the way a little kid would, and sat down at the piano and played the first few chords of "Blue Monk." Everybody thought that the music was coming over the audio system, hey, somebody put on Monk, and it took a few minutes before anybody even noticed the skinny white chick at the keyboard, wailing, wailing on some old upbeat Bud Powell tune, and then, by the time the last stragglers and the bartenders and the drummer and bass player from the group that had just finished playing had gathered around the piano, Billie was already deep into a medley of Gil Evans tunes and wrecking, and I mean wrecking, any chance that anything else that had happened that night to anyone listening would stay in their memories. It wasn't like the way it happens in the movies. The bass player didn't pick up his instrument and start to lay down a line behind her, the drummer didn't set up his kit again and begin to kick her further along. They just stood there, until the sun came up, nodding their heads, and the next afternoon started talking about her and what she had done. She was a freak, she was a skinny little Jewish bitch, she was a white girl with powers, she was underage, and when word got around about her impromptu early morning set, she became a mystery and a legend.

Her mother was the one responsible for her first union card. She had a client who knew somebody—a lot of her clients knew people who could do these things—and that somebody told somebody else to do something, so before she graduated from high school, before she could legally taste a drink in any of these clubs, Billie was playing concerts, and as soon as she turned twenty-one she dropped out of college before graduating—maybe I wouldn't talk about this part with Ceely—and started playing the clubs. Before long she had her own trio—that same bass man and drummer who were the first witnesses to her prowess that early morning in New York.

Her mother, your grandmother, well, I don't want to wail too hard on her, because I know you love her and your grandfather, and to be honest if they hadn't been there after your mother and I split I don't know what we would have done. Billie was out on the road a lot that year, she had a lot of international festivals to play, Osaka and Copenhagen, places like that, which is what brought everything crashing down on our heads. I don't know if she ever told you about any of it, and you were probably too young to digest much of it anyway. But she called me from one of her concert trips, from Amsterdam, to be precise. And she told me over the telephone, in a voice clear as a bell (and I knew she wasn't stoned or drunk), that it was over with us. I didn't want to think about where she was calling from, from whose hotel room, the bass player's? from the room of the young horn player they added for the tour? I could just tell that somebody was standing near her, though I never did know many of the

exact details, I didn't want to know, and to help me remain ignorant I started drinking a lot, and this didn't help you much, dear
child, waking in the middle of the night crying for your mother
only to be comforted by a father sobbing over you, spraying you
with his whiskey breath. Just as quickly as she had taken up with
me, she had broken off with me.

I don't know why she came to despise me so, and I
guess I never really want to know. I forgive her everything,
because she did try, as best she could, to be a good mother to
you. One of the first things that happened after she called me
was that her mother called.

"I heard," she said.

It only took me a week to figure out that I had to bring
you up there to Manhattan.

Your grandmother had already arranged for a nanny,
Mrs. Griggs. Devoted to you until the day that she died.

All those years that you lived with them, with your
mother coming and going like a bee back and forth from the
hive, making her reputation, trying to raise you, thank God for
your grandparents and Mrs. Griggs, right? I'll never know until
you tell me what went through your mind, not anything anyone
can really tell about until they get to a certain age anyway, at
least I wouldn't have been able to talk about it, the way I felt
when I was growing up. Here you were, an only child, living
with your grandparents, though certainly never wanting for any
luxury, let alone necessity, the best clothes, the best food, the
best schools, fancy friends, all those musicians your mother
introduced you to, the inner circle of the inner circle of modern
jazz, concerts and festivals (and I know she sneaked you into a
few bars, too, don't deny it). You had piano lessons from the best
teachers, classical and jazz, you had dance classes, you knew the

best museums inside out, you got to know a lot about the criminal justice system, rubbing elbows at dinners sometimes with mobsters, sometimes with judges, and you got a little education in philosophy from your grandfather who talked to you about Aristotle and Plato and Kant and Kierkegaard as though they were men he saw at his club. (Yes, club, the money, the huge apartment on Park Avenue, Billie grew up the same way, with the best, nothing but the best.) But what it was like for you, what it felt like, that's what I want to talk to you about, because seeing you on my weekly visits I could scarcely get a sense of how you felt except that you seemed comfortable with everything, it wasn't as if you disliked the way you were living, but the feeling of it, that's what I'm interested in, that's the one thing we never talked about, because at first you were too young and then when you got older you were too busy, with friends, with school.

It's just that I never really liked your grandparents, a feeling that I picked up, I suppose, from things Billie said about them. Your grandfather, a brilliant thinker and one of the most handsome men, in his own short dark Jewish way, on the faculty, your grandmother, known in judicial circles as the Bitch, because if she had a case she wanted to fight for, and that was usually just about any case she took on, she went no holds barred against the prosecutors, sometimes the police, and every now and then a judge.

"Once she was cited for contempt," I remember Billie saying, "that clicked for me. I held her in contempt for ever after that. Such a hypocrite, once I got to know who she was, I couldn't bear to be around her. The way she encouraged my music, until I turned to jazz. The way she upheld the rights of the downtrodden, if they could come up with a million dollar fee. And race, on race, she was a real bitch. All sweetness and light about the scholarship kids, which meant the dark-skinned kids, at school.

And then I started hanging out with them. Until that happened, I thought my father was pretty much a stand-up guy. I mean, he could tell you more than you wanted to know about Kierkegaard and Sartre and folks like that. Sometimes he would go off into his study and not come out except for meals. When my mother started wailing on me, he stayed in that study for days. I went in there one time looking for him and he was gone, I didn't even hear him leave the apartment. He went to teach, I guess. Or maybe some place else. I just happened to take a look at some of the things on his desk and found a couple of notes from another woman that scared the hell out of me. But then, I figured, if I was married to my mother, I would need somebody else to comfort me, too."

(Your mother could talk for a long time about all the hurts, especially when she was high and believed that if she tried hard enough she could see a light behind the visible that wasn't always normally apparent. That's what made her music so special, that transcendental quality about it, even in the simplest tunes.)

But your grandparents were terrific with you after your mother and I split up, right up until her death. Of course they couldn't help with what you were feeling inside, though you wouldn't know you were so troubled, you sleeping so peacefully as we drive south, the entire length of the New Jersey Turnpike now behind us as we rise up on the roadway of the Delaware Memorial Bridge, almost like soaring in a glider or small airplane, the hazy horizon stretching out on either side, the river below, it's been hours and hours, morning has become afternoon and now late afternoon, and I'm quite exhausted myself, the long drive up, the night rendered nearly sleepless because of the noisy couple in the next room. I could shut my eyes now, I should pull over and shut my eyes, except that I'm thinking about my own fatigue, and suddenly I'm wondering if there might be something wrong with you, you slept through a stop for gas, you slept through a stop for coffee, and just as I'm really beginning to worry, as we pass through the toll gate and head south toward Baltimore you turn to one side and then the other, and then you open your eyes.

"Hi."

"Hi."

"You really went out."

"This whole thing has made me exhausted. This whole life."

"I'm sorry you're so upset, sweetheart."

"Oh, it's nothing, just my mother, dead from heroin."

"I don't think you should—"

"Should what, Dad? Should this? Should that? Should anything? I should have just set myself completely on fire and been done with it."

"Like some Indian widow? She was your mother, not your husband."

She gave me a look, and I had to look away, which was a good idea at the time anyway since I would have missed the right curve of the road off in the Baltimore direction. So though she was awake we drove for a while in silence into the thickening air of late afternoon. Delaware. The toll booth at the Delaware Turnpike. I paid the toll and we passed on through and drove a while longer.

Ceely seemed to be studying the scenery, the woods and fields, the sun which now was heading for a low point in the western sky, the sky itself. Then she turned to the dashboard and fiddled with the CD player.

Fire, light, day, the moon's brightness,
the six months of the north-turning sun...

"What is this again?"

I told her, adding that I didn't know much about it.

These paths, of light and of darkness,
have always existed; by one
a man will escape from rebirth...

Traffic all of a sudden seemed to be bunching up, though we were still traveling at a good sixty miles an hour. Tired as I was, I strained to keep my attention on the road.

"Okay, Father," Ceely said.

"Okay?"

"Let's talk."

That was when this next thing happened, all the cars ahead of us jammed but not slowing down, something going on up ahead. If I just tell you what occurred in the time that it took for it to happen it went by as quickly as it takes for you to hear this. The dogs! Instant terror! And the falling off as they disappeared behind us. But I'll slow it down, so you can see the danger a little more clearly, a pack of dogs, four or five large animals running toward us between and alongside the cars, dogs running so fast and in such great bounds forward, shepherds, I think they were, but our glimpse of them was so brief that they might well have been some other breed, none of the cars swerving, ours included, just the dogs running forward between us—and then they were gone, leaving me shaking at the wheel.

"Jesus," Ceely said, looking around behind us.

"See them?" I said, scarcely able to catch my breath.

"They're gone," she said.

"We should all be dead," I said, still fighting for air.

"But we're not, father," Ceely said, "we're not." And there was something new and terribly admirable in her voice that almost made me forget about my instant terror and the way that my breath became so difficult to rehearse.

3—The Exorcism

So, Erna, that was all several months ago, and a lot of things, mostly good, have happened since then.

Beginning with Charmaine waiting with dinner for us the night we arrived. And, after we had installed Ceely in the guest room and closed up the house, saying to me in bed, "I want you to forgive me for making you think I didn't want her here."

"Nothing to forgive," I said. I was still a little shaky from the road, still thinking about those dogs.

"I was feeling jealous, and I feel stupid about that," she said. "She's not Billie. I shouldn't think of her as Billie."

"No, you shouldn't," I said. "I don't."

"Of course not," Charmaine said. "Of course not."

I took a deep breath and tried to slough off all of the cares and tremors of the last day and a half.

"Tell me," I said, "how did you come to see things this way?"

"I went for a healing session last week with an incredible woman named Erna, someone Dr. Gordon recommended to me."

"A healing session? Maybe I should go to one."

"Maybe you should," Charmaine said. "But first we've got to help Ceely."

So, the next day, we got Ceely an appointment to see Dr. Gordon, a psychiatrist whom Charmaine knew from the days of her herbal business. I don't know what transpired in their twice-weekly appointments, but something was going on. Soon after the burns on her hand began to heal, Ceely started talking with us at dinner, about all the love and misery of being her mother's daughter, about how sorry she felt for her grandparents, the way they lived—"all that money and all those brains, and they don't have a clue"—her love for certain courses at school, her insecurities with her friends, her doubts about her lovers and the possibility of love. I walked around the house when she wasn't there—she found a part-time job at a local coffee house—shaking my head in astonishment.

Rashid came down for a visit and that gave me all the more fuel for amazement.

In a miraculous burst of empathy, Charmaine and I agreed almost without discussion that we wouldn't say a word when Ceely took his bag into her room and assumed that they would share it for the length of his stay. In a miraculous burst of insight, Ceely told Rashid that he would sleep on the living room sofa and could use her bathroom in the guest room.

He didn't stay for very long. I never heard any evidence of discord between them—certainly not while lying in bed awake the first night of his stay, wondering what was going on downstairs, and absolutely not when I climbed stealthily out of bed and tip-toed down the stairs more than halfway to listen to their voices over the quiet insistence of the music from Ceely's stereo (the best I could build her, by the way).

"It's not that," Ceely was saying.

"Then what was it?" Rashid's voice was up in the higher registers, a nervous voice, the voice of a fellow who has traveled some distance only to discover he's not going to get what he wants to get (in other words, a fellow I understood perfectly, as most men would, since I had been there before him, and so, despite my natural response to him, which was jealousy and anger for hanging around my precious daughter, I forgave him, I did, I did).

"I just need some time," she said.

Rashid said something that I couldn't quite make out, but whose tone I recognized.

"I can't help it," she said. "…what I've been through."

"Sure, girl," he said. "And what about me?"

Erna, could she have discovered so much insight into her life at such an early age? I never had it at that time of my life. I was so ignorant as to have proposed marriage to her mother, and her mother, for all of the tough exterior she acquired at such an early age because of her budding jazz life, was just as ignorant, and innocent. I forgive her. I may have said this before, but I'll say it again, I forgive her.

After a fairly pleasant dinner with all of us the next evening, Rashid was gone.

"Are you all right?" I asked Ceely after he went out the door.

"I'm fine," she said, holding up her nearly healed hand for me to see.

"I didn't mean just that," I said.

"This is a sign," she said. "The hand. It stands for other things."

That was lovely. Everybody was in good shape, healing. Charmaine. Ceely. Even her grandparents, whom she visited for a few days soon after Rashid departed.

"No trouble?" I said to her over the telephone.

"They're being very sweet to me," Ceely said. "We had a nice dinner tonight. So what's up with you, Father?" She sounded so right, so normal.

"I wish I could explain." Well, I didn't actually say that. But I was thinking it.

I couldn't get to sleep that night, dog after dog after dog ran between the lanes in my restless thoughts, and in my mind's ear, I could hear the sweet screeching of a violin played by that concertmistress from Seattle. My tossing and turning finally woke Charmaine.

"What is it?" she said.

I surprised myself by bursting into tears.

"What?" she said, taking me in her arms as though I were just one big baby.

"Everybody's getting better," I said. "Except me. I'm fucking worthless. I can't get close to you. I can't get close to Ceely. Maybe I should just kill myself!" And I lapsed into another terrible round of weeping and sobbing. I shook. She shook. The bed shook.

"Look," she said. It took her a while to explain to me what she thought I needed to look at, and a while before I could face up to what she said. But—and I mean this with no disrespect, because it was just the way that I saw things before I met you, Erna—I was so desperate I would try anything, and so she finally had me convinced. In the middle of the night I decided to cancel a trip to Seattle where I was supposed to do a check on the rock and roll museum and lay about the house while Ceely spent another week or more in New York City.

I was lying on the sofa—it was the day you had kindly arranged for me to fill a hole in your busy schedule of treatments—reading the front page of the newspaper over and over again, Charmaine out at her shop, the early spring sun lighting the eastern part of the sunroom, when the telephone rang. I was wallowing in the terrible funk of a man too timid to admit that he was in desperate trouble. It was all I could do to get up and answer the call.

"Hello?"

Woman's voice, low and familiar at the other end of the line.

"Good morning, Mr. Swanson."

It was one of those moments, when the caller doesn't identify herself because she believes that you will know who she is.

"Hi," I said.

"How are you?"

"Fine," I said. It was maddening, I knew the voice but just couldn't place it.

"And Ceely?"

"Ceely?"

Ah, it was the dean! The dean!

I told her about Ceely's therapy, and that her hand was healing. She was making progress, yes.

"It sounds as though things are going well. Will you be bringing her back next term?"

"That's up to you, isn't it? Will you reinstate her?"

"We'll hold her place, yes. When the time gets closer, perhaps you can get her therapist to write a letter for her."

"Okay. But what about the bill? The damage to the piano?"

"Oh, I think our insurance will cover that."

"Thank you."

"But you might call me to double-check about that. And come in to see me when you bring her back. I like to talk with parents face to face. You have my number."

"Yes," I said.

"You understand?"

I thought I did. So I said yes, I did.

But I didn't know if I did.

I walked—though it felt like crawling—back to the sofa where I had left the newspaper.

I picked it up and read the first section yet again. But a vision of me and the dean locked in a fornicator's embrace kept coming between me and the page. That odd smile of hers. A certain quality to her voice. I lay there wallowing in the fantasy, a tepid bath in sullied water.

And then it was time for me to go.

Erna, your office in the basement of the building where Dr. Gordon had his medical practice was wonderfully quiet, and that appealed to the technician in me. Once I arrived and closed the door behind me, the traffic on Connecticut Avenue was hardly a whisper in my ears. I listened to the flow and clicks of the room itself, to the unnoise made by the air and the light. You came in, wrapped in silence yourself, in your old blue sweater and peasant skirt, something that you probably wore for years while still working in Brazil. Your clothes and your quiet manner made it possible for me to stay calm in the face of what part of me understood to be an outrageous undertaking.

"You're nervous," you said in your accented English. If I didn't know you were Brazilian, living here for about five years (Charmaine filled me in with the details), I might have taken you for Romanian or Hungarian, your voice had that sort of lilt and plushy swerve.

"Kind of," I said, and followed your instructions, removing my shoes and lying on my back on the long treatment table in the center of the room. You dimmed the overhead lights and approached the table and began to speak. Your voice was low, and your breath tinged slightly with cigarette smoke.

"You have worries, yes?"

"I do, I do."

"Tell me your worries."

This was a little embarrassing. I said some cursory things about Ceely, and about Charmaine. All the while you were tracing my body with your hands a few inches in the air above me.

"And about your work, do you have worries?"

"Not so much anymore," I said. "When I was younger, yes."

"But now you feel secure in it?"

"Pretty much."

"So it is just your family."

"Yes," I said.

"The living and the dead," you said.

"Yes. What do you mean?"

"You know what I mean," you said.

"Billie?" I said.

"Who is Billie?"

I told you a little about her.

"Yes," you said, having known without knowing, and now knowing without having known.

It was at this point that I began to think this was either all a big hoax, or a big wonder.

"Are you ready now?" you said.

"I suppose so," I said.

"Do you understand that I will say a little prayer before I begin? That is just the way I do things."

"Yes, my wife told me," I said.

"I call on Jesus. And I call on St. Michael and all his holy minions to come into your body, these heavenly entities enter you and cleanse you of the earthbound spirits that weigh your body down."

"I see."

"You sound fearful. You musn't be fearful. There is no harm that can come to you through this, only good."

"I need some good," I said, trying to laugh.

"You may feel things. You may see lights. Other things happen to other people."

"Okay," I said.

"And when it is over, you will make a list for me."

"Okay. What kind of list?"

"Of everyone you wish to forgive for all of the wrongs and hurts they have done to you. Do you understand? You'll write it down and bring it to me."

"I do," I said. "I'll write it down."

"Good. But you must also be on guard."

"On guard?"

"The wandering earthbound entities, the ones who take over your internal organs and make for disease and bad thoughts and bad decisions, they will flee, but then they will also try to come back in."

"I'll be on guard," I said.

"You must," she said.

"I will," I said.

"Then we will begin."

I swallowed, tried to calm myself. But my heart beat hard, and I blinked, and blinked, and finally closed my eyes.

"In the name of Jesus and all the saints," you said. "Michael, Saint Michael, come to me and attend us, enter into the body of this man, down, down, down, with all of your helpers, and all of the hundreds, thousands of you, build the light about his head, build the light about his body, make it increase and flow and burn away…"

You talked, you chanted, you whispered, you said a crown of light would appear above my head, and I felt it, and it increased, and it ran down and up the length of my body as I breathed and breathed as hard as if I were rowing in a race, and you said that hundreds, perhaps thousands of entities would enter my body and cleanse it of illness and trouble and distress and worry and woe, down, down, down past the molecular level to the subatomic level and even beneath that, and you had me breathe harder and I rushed and I huffed and I hushed and I felt the heat from your hands hovering above me and I saw light gathering before my lidded eyes—and, sound man that I am, I heard horns, trumpets, I heard loud oaths and the clank and clash of metal on metal on wood and bone and I smelled burning wood and burning flesh, and my body began to tremble, as if I had a terrible fever, though I felt nothing but gentle fire and saw only a gathering of light before my closed eyes, and then I felt as though I were floating off the table, and then, like silk gently falling, settling back onto the table, and I heard the very noise of the molecules gathering and spinning and whirling and dancing. And these were worlds careening and turning in space without limits, and the sound of the essence of existence was both grand and small, from the biggest boom of cataclysmic explosion to the tiniest whisper of the rustle of the fluttering eyelash or the sweet resolve of the falling leaf.

Oh, Erna, I knew my soul, and it knew me, and I had done bad things and I had done good, and time opened out to me now, the way a door opens onto a new room or a shade slips up and I could see, oh, I could see what I had done and what had to be done for this time and time to come. This was life, I said to myself in my own voice, this was life on Earth, on this planet turning endlessly in a solar system captive of a turning galaxy that was moving itself toward some goal grander than anything any of us might imagine. And I heard music, more music, drum and bass, and the piano coming up under it, flirting with the rhythms and then molding them to its own forward charge, angels playing jazz, angel jazz, and my heart sprung loose, and the blues poured out—Jew blues, black blues, Lutheran blues, half blues, all blues—and I wept, and wept, and more than wept, cleansing my soul, and wept again.

I went home humming "Jew-Bop," hooleeyou-do, da-da-dat, hooleeyou-do, dat-da-da..." and when Charmaine came home I had dinner ready and flowers to present to her.

"How was it?" she said.

"Amazing," I said.

That night we talked of how you, with the help of St. Michael and all of his minions, had purged me of my hurts and my woes and my pains and my false desires, and we talked of many other things as well, old loves and new, and rejuvenating former affections and keeping the good memories in our hearts. In the middle of our conversation, barefoot and in my undershirt, I ran out to the car and fetched the CD and played parts of the Gita for her—

> *Fire, light, day, the moon's brightness,*
> *the six months of the north-turning sun…*

Oh, my God, the beauty of it all, the poetry, yes, yes, yes, yes, fire, light, day, the moon's brightness, the taste of the water, the six months of the north-turning sun, heat, sparks, flames, whirl, I was a man waylaid by demons, by earth-bound entities, as all men are, but I saw an end to it, I knew I had a chance, I knew that I must change my life! I felt that, I felt it rising in my heart!

Ceely called late to say that she was coming home the next afternoon. She had talked to some of her grandparents' friends, she might have a job in New York. That was wonderful news. She would recover. She might even find some direction. There was hope, for her, and even for me, was how I felt. And then I turned to Charmaine, and we made good love and slept pressed close to each other, the way survivors on a life-raft might after a wreck at sea. I woke up only once, to hear the sharp, harsh, ratchety music of neighborhood dogs barking in the distant dark.

And then very early in the morning I backslid, I confess—and I hope you'll forgive me—that I wasn't completely exorcised—because I stole down the stairs, assailed by chill air when there should have been none, and called the dean at home.

"Jackie?" she said.

I hung up the receiver.

It's just, as they say in some stories, that I had a moment of recognition. The rest of the day slipped by and I have very little recollection of what it was like except that

I began writing the list of all of those people whom I want to forgive.

It was early evening already when Ceely arrived at Union Station and called to tell me that she was taking the Metro here.

"I'll pick you up at the Metro stop," I said.

"That's okay, Father," she said. "I can walk."

"I'll be there," I said.

Smoke, gloom, night, the moon's darkness,
the six months of the south-turning sun...

I listened for a moment to the *Gita* as I drove down to the Metro stop, but then turned it off. It was beautiful poetry, but I still had my life to live, didn't I? The cycles of things, birth and death and rebirth, all of that took second place right now to some practical business. Sitting behind the wheel of a car, watching, waiting, while traffic rolled around me in the fading light. A number of people emerged from the exit, men with briefcases, women in pants suits, a mother with child, a few teenage girls with short haircuts, a tall black man arm in arm with a rotund woman who might have been his mother. Here is life, I said to myself in that fuzzy muddled way we have of trying to tell ourselves that we are attentive to the world when actually we are dreaming.

I looked away at the sound of a passing bus. Minutes went by, and more minutes. Where was she? How had I missed her! My own daughter!

Oh, St. Michael, you and all your minions, I finally left the Metro exit and drove around the block. Halfway up the street, I saw a tall girl hurrying along with a backpack much like Ceely's. But she had short hair, very short, I noticed, as I slowed down and passed her by.

"Hey!" she waved at me.

I stopped the car. It was Ceely. Nearly bald.

"What do you think?" she said when she climbed into the car. "Neat, huh? Grandma took a day off from court to take me to the hairdresser. She treated me."

Her face glowed despite the onset of the dark, and as though a fire burned within the center of her skull her scalp showed nearly pink through the stubble of her hair. By that light I saw myself, as I once had been, as I was now, as I might be tomorrow, nothing but a sound man detached from his problems, but the only father she would ever have.

In one of those wonderful slips of the tongue in which the truth slides out like a child in easy birth, I said, "I forgive me."

Ceely gave me a beatific smile, humming something I recognized as one of her mother's tunes, and I steered us the rest of the way home.

Acknowledgements

The author gratefully acknowledges Mitch Wieland and the fiction staff of *The Idaho Review,* where these novellas first appeared.

Lines from the *Bhagavad Gita,* translated by Stephen Mitchell, copyright ©2000 by Stephen Mitchell, used by permission of Harmony Books, a division of Random House, Inc.

NEIL ADAMS, GEORGE MASON UNIVERSITY

About the Author

Alan Cheuse is the author of three novels, including *The Grandmothers' Club* and *The Light Possessed,* three collections of short stories, a memoir *Fall Out of Heaven,* and a collection of essays, *Listening to the Page: Adventures in Reading and Writing.* Recently, his short fiction has appeared in *Ploughshares, The Antioch Review, New Letters, Prairie Schooner,* and *The Southern Review.* He is the editor of the anthology *Seeing Ourselves: Great Stories of America's Past* and co-editor of *Writers Workshop in a Book: The Squaw Valley Community of Writers on the Art of Fiction.* Cheuse serves as book commentator for NPR's "All Things Considered" and as a member of the writing faculty at George Mason University.

www.alancheuse.com